What did she do?

Did she give in to the almost overwhelming attraction and kiss him?

If she gave in, it wouldn't exactly be orthodox, but then again, it wasn't as if Lucas Wingate was her patient. It was his daughter she'd treated, and this was really a social visit, not a professional one. She was here as a "friend," not a doctor.

So what are you going to do? You can't just stand here forever like some statue. Do something.

And then, to Nikki's overwhelming relief and surprise, the ultimate decision was taken away from her. Lucas freed her of the responsibility.

Slipping his hands into her hair and framing her face with a movement as soft and as gentle as a whisper, Lucas touched his lips to hers.

Dear Reader,

Someone once said that the definition of a sweater was something you wore when your mother was cold. And, in keeping with that, the definition of a mother is someone who only wants the best for you—no matter how crazy that makes you.

Since the beginning of time, mothers have meddled in their children's lives. Children, I'm sure they all feel, need the guidance of someone older and wiser, someone who's already been through this tricky part of life. I've been on both sides of the fence and neither is easy. But it can be amusing (especially if it's happening to someone else). The MATCHMAKING MAMAS miniseries is about three such mothers, lifelong friends who have daughters and absolutely no prospects of becoming grandmothers in the near, or far, future. They decide to take matters into their own hands, subtly if possible, and push their daughters in the right direction. Nothing but good things can come of this, right? Of course right. Maybe. Come judge for yourself.

I hope you enjoy this lighthearted peek into the very special relationship of stubborn mothers and resisting daughters. If it brings a smile to your lips, I've done my job.

I wish you love and the best of everything.

Marie Ferrarella

DOCTORING THE SINGLE DAD

MARIE FERRARELLA

Silhouette®

SPECIAL EDITION®

Published by Silhouette Books

America's Publisher of Contemporary Romance

If you purchased this book without a cover you should be aware that this book is stolen property. It was reported as "unsold and destroyed" to the publisher, and neither the author nor the publisher has received any payment for this "stripped book."

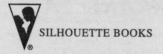

SILHOUETTE BOOKS

Recycling programs for this product may not exist in your area.

ISBN-13: 978-0-373-65513-7

DOCTORING THE SINGLE DAD

Copyright © 2010 by Marie Rydzynski-Ferrarella

All rights reserved. Except for use in any review, the reproduction or utilization of this work in whole or in part in any form by any electronic, mechanical or other means, now known or hereafter invented, including xerography, photocopying and recording, or in any information storage or retrieval system, is forbidden without the written permission of the editorial office, Silhouette Books, 233 Broadway, New York, NY 10279 U.S.A.

This is a work of fiction. Names, characters, places and incidents are either the product of the author's imagination or are used fictitiously, and any resemblance to actual persons, living or dead, business establishments, events or locales is entirely coincidental.

This edition published by arrangement with Harlequin Books S.A.

For questions and comments about the quality of this book please contact us at Customer_eCare@Harlequin.ca.

® and TM are trademarks of Harlequin Books S.A., used under license. Trademarks indicated with ® are registered in the United States Patent and Trademark Office, the Canadian Trade Marks Office and in other countries.

Visit Silhouette Books at www.eHarlequin.com

Printed in U.S.A.

Books by Marie Ferrarella

MARIE FERRARELLA

This *USA TODAY* bestselling and RITA® Award-winning author has written almost two hundred novels for Silhouette Books, some under the name Marie Nicole. Her romances are beloved by fans worldwide. Visit her Web site at www.marieferrarella.com.

This book is dedicated
to every mother
who has ever uttered,
"But darling, it's not really a setup...."

Prologue

"**Y**ou're frowning," Theresa Manetti commented to Maizie Sommers. "What's wrong?"

Maizie was one of her two oldest best friends and she, Maizie and Cecilia Parnell, the *other* best friend in their trio were playing poker as they did every week— come hell or high water—for years now.

Maizie put the cards she was holding facedown on the table and shook her head. Her short, cropped, silvery platinum straight hair swung back and forth, underlining her feelings. Her clear blue eyes snapped as she said, "I don't feel like playing poker."

"All right," Theresa said gamely, "what do you feel like doing?"

Maizie's answer was simple. "Screaming."

Theresa and Cecilia exchanged looks. They suddenly knew where this was heading. Lifelong friends, they had been together since the third grade when tall, gangly Michael Fitzpatrick had stolen a kiss from a very startled Theresa. He'd gotten decked for his trouble when Cecilia and Maizie—predominantly Maizie—had chased him down and cornered him at the end of the schoolyard. Maizie did most of the swinging. Victim, perpetrator and erstwhile defenders had all gotten one week of detention for causing the disruption, at the end of which three of them became fast friends while Michael made plans to eventually join the Jesuits.

Maizie, Theresa and Cecilia attended the same schools, went away to the same college and were in each other's bridal parties. Moreover, they stood by one another through all the joyous events, like the birth of each other's children. They were no less steadfast during the sorrowful events, as one by one, they all became widows long before their time. And when Theresa, as a young mother of two, faced the specter of breast cancer, Maizie and Cecilia were the ones who took over the daily chores and lifted the spirits of her worried husband and children.

After so many years together, the three knew each other as well as they knew their own minds. Which was why they sensed that the source of Maizie's angst was her daughter, Nicole. Both women could relate to what their friend was going through. They both had single daughters.

Cecilia broached the subject first. "It's Nikki, isn't it?"

"Of course it's Nikki. Do you know what she said to me?"

"No," Cecilia replied. "But I'm sure you're going to tell us."

"She actually said that if she never got married, she was fine with that. Can you imagine that?" Maizie cried.

Theresa sighed. "Kate said almost the same thing the other day."

Cecilia added her voice to the concert. "Must be something going around. The last time we talked, Jewel told me that she was 'happy' with her life the way it was. I know I should be happy that she's happy, but—"

"You know what this means, don't you?" Maizie asked the others.

"Yes, that we're never going to have any grandchildren." There was a catch in Theresa's voice as she made the daunting prediction.

Maizie leaned over the table, placing one hand on each of her friends' hands. "All right, what are we going to do about this?"

"Do?" Theresa repeated, confused. "What can we do? I mean, it's not like the girls are twelve."

"Of course not," Maizie scoffed. "If they were twelve, we wouldn't be worrying about them never getting married, would we?"

"I think Theresa means that they're adult women," Cecilia said.

The argument held no water for Maizie. "So, you

stop being a mother because there're more than twenty-one candles on the cake?"

"Of course not," Theresa protested. "I'll always be Kate's mother, but—"

Maizie seized the word. "We've been sitting a little too long on our butts. It's time we shook things up a little bit."

"What are you talking about, Maizie?" Theresa asked.

"Maizie's just frustrated, Theresa—" Cecilia got no further.

"Of course I'm frustrated. And you are, too. I know you." She looked from one woman to the other. "When we were the same age as the girls are now, we were married with a baby on the way."

"Times are different these days, Maizie," Theresa began.

"Not so different," Maizie maintained. "Love still makes the world go around. Don't you want your girls to find love?"

"Of course we do," Cecilia declared. "But it's beginning to look like, short of some kind of divine intervention, that's just not going to happen."

"Read the newspaper, Cecilia. God's a little busy right now. Besides," Maizie looked at Theresa for support. "He helps those who help themselves, right?"

"Right," Theresa agreed slowly, then asked a bit uneasily, "Just exactly what are you getting at?"

"I know that smile." Cecilia pointed at Maizie. "That's the smile Bette Davis wore in *All About Eve* when she told everyone at the party to buckle up because it was going to be a bumpy night."

Maizie laughed. "No bumpy anything. All I'm saying is that it wasn't that long ago when parents arranged marriages for their children." There was skepticism on Theresa's face. "Why are you looking at me like that?"

"If you ask me, *you* need help if you think this has any chance of flying, Maizie. I don't know about Nikki, but if Kate was any more independent, she'd be her own country."

"Jewel's the same way," Cecilia agreed. "She balks at blind dates or being set up. Believe me, *I have tried.* I guarantee the girls are just not going to go for whatever it is that you have in mind, Maizie."

"Who says we have to tell them?" Maizie asked innocently.

"Okay, spill it," Cecilia demanded. "Just what are you up to?"

"Oh c'mon, ladies, *think,*" Maizie urged. "We've each got our own companies. We interact with a host of people everyday. *Different* people," she emphasized. "I've got my own real-estate company, you have a catering business—" She waved a hand at Theresa. "And you have a cleaning service—"

"We all know what we have," Cecilia cut in. "What does all that have to do with getting Nikki, Kate and Jewel married?"

"We're all in a position to keep our eyes opened for prospects," Maizie insisted with enthusiasm.

Theresa looked at Cecilia. "You know what she's talking about?"

Before Cecilia could respond, Maizie underscored, "Unmarried, eligible men, Theresa. There're more single men out there than ever," she cried. "We're in the perfect vocations to meet them."

"And what, we lasso one if we like what we see and bring him home to the girls?" Cecilia asked sarcastically.

"There are laws against that, Maizie," Theresa said quietly.

"There are no laws against using your brain and setting things up," Maizie insisted. "Don't just look at them as clients, look at them as men. As potential sons-in-law," she stressed.

"All right, pretend that we're going along with this," Cecilia conceded. "What if one of us actually sees a 'potential' son-in-law, then what?"

Maizie's eyes danced. "Then we improvise. We're all clever women. We can do this. Desperate times call for desperate measures," she reminded them. Satisfied that she had gotten them to consider her idea, she relaxed and smiled. "Now," she looked from one friend to another as she rubbed her hands together, definitely more buoyant than she had been a few minutes ago, "What do you say we play a little poker? Suddenly, I'm feeling very lucky."

Theresa and Cecilia exchanged looks. The idea was crazy enough to work. At least, it was worth a try.

Chapter One

Maizie decided to give her daughter one more chance to redeem herself before she went ahead with her plan.

Because she knew how busy her pediatrician daughter was, what with her own practice and volunteering at the free clinic twice a month, Maizie made Nikki her favorite meal, the same meal her late husband had loved, and brought it over to her daughter's house.

She forgot to take Nikki's unpredictable schedule into account and wound up waiting almost an hour before Nikki pulled up in her driveway.

Surprised to see her mother leaning against the door, a dark blue casserole dish at her feet, Nikki rolled down her window. The breeze playfully blew her light blonde hair into her mouth. Pushing the now damp strand aside, she called out, "Were we on for tonight?" Parking quickly, she got out of the vehicle.

Maizie bent down to pick up the casserole dish and said cheerfully, "No, this is just an impromptu visit."

Eyes the same shade of blue as her mother's now scrutinized Maizie. Her mother had stopped popping up in her life unannounced right after she graduated medical school. Nikki wondered what was up. "Sorry if I kept you waiting," she apologized. "Have you been here long?"

"No, not long," Maizie lied.

Nikki glanced at the casserole dish her mother was holding. *Beware of mothers bearing gifts.*

Unlocking her front door, Nikki held it open for her mother as the latter walked in and began to make her way to the kitchen. There was something a little too cheerful, a little too innocent about her mother tonight, she thought. And then it came to her.

"You played poker with Aunt Cecilia and Aunt Theresa, didn't you?" Nikki asked, closing the door again. She flipped the lock.

"I play with them every week, dear," Maizie answered innocently.

The game was just an excuse for gossiping, exchanging information and comparing notes. "I know what goes on at those games, Mom."

Setting the casserole down on the table, Maizie placed her hand to her chest and dramatically cried,

"Oh my Lord, I certainly hope not. I wouldn't want to be the one who got those poor men arrested."

"Men?" Nikki reached into the cupboard and took out two dinner plates. "What men?" Taking out the silverware, she glanced over her shoulder at her mother. "What are you talking about?"

Maizie took the glass lid off the casserole dish. "Why, the ones who play strip poker with us, of course," she deadpanned. "What other men would I be talking about?"

Putting the plates on the table, Nikki took out two glasses, then got a soda can out of the refrigerator. "Mother, you are crazy, you know that, don't you?"

Maizie took the glasses from her daughter and placed them next to the plates. "I'm not crazy, but if I was, no one could blame me for going that route. Loneliness does that to a person."

"Loneliness? Ha! Mom, I've seen perfect strangers come up to you and just start talking, pouring out their hearts." As far back as she could remember, her mother had always had that kind of face. A face that encouraged people to talk to her even though they didn't know her. Her mother did nothing to discourage them.

Maizie shrugged. "They don't count. And they weren't that perfect."

"And what does count?" Nikki knew in her heart where this was going. Where all her conversations with her mother eventually went. To the nursery. "Babies?"

"Yes!" Maizie cried with feeling.

"Fine," Nikki said with a straight face, "you can

come to work with me tomorrow, mingle with all the babies you want."

Maizie's smile vanished. "Those are other people's babies."

"Same thing. They're still babies," Nikki told her, taking a handful of napkins and depositing them on the table between the two plates.

"No, it's not the same thing," Maizie insisted. "Are you satisfied just holding other people's babies? Don't you want a baby of your own to hold, Nikki? Don't you want a baby of your own to love and care for?"

Nikki rolled her eyes. They'd danced this dance before. Many times. "Yes, Mother, I want one of my own and if it's meant to be, it'll happen," Nikki assured her. "In the meantime," she continued, sitting down and pulling her chair closer to the table, "I'm doing something good. Mom, I love you more than anything in this world, but please, give it a rest."

Maizie shook her head sadly. "It's been resting too long."

"Not by my count," Nikki said pointedly. She was determined to change the subject. "C'mon, Mom," she urged. "Let's just eat and enjoy each other's company." She indicated the uncovered casserole. "The stew smells really good."

"It smells really cold," Maizie contradicted. "I was waiting for an hour."

"I thought you said you weren't waiting all that long."

"I lied. One of the few times," Maizie was quick to add.

"Right." Nikki let that slide, choosing instead to explain why she was late. "Mrs. Lee went into early labor. This was her first baby and she didn't have a pediatrician. Larry called me just as I was leaving the office."

Maizie instantly became alert. "Larry? Larry Bishop?"

Too late. Nikki realized the minefield she'd just walked into. She and the ob-gyn had dated for a few months. Until she discovered that Larry's idea of exclusive dating meant that she dated *him* exclusively and he dated anyone he wanted to.

"Yes, Mother," she answered patiently, "Larry Bishop."

"How is Larry these days?" her mother prodded.

"Engaged," Nikki responded, taking the casserole dish and bringing it over to the microwave. She set the dial for three minutes.

Maizie shifted around in her chair. "Permanently?" she asked.

"No, I imagine one of these days, he'll get tired of being engaged and get married." *And I feel sorry for his wife,* she added silently. Nikki turned away from the oven and leaned her back against the counter. "Don't frown like that, Mom. Didn't Grandma tell you that your face'll freeze that way if you're not careful?" she teased with a straight face.

"She might have, but I was too busy taking care of *my baby,*" Maizie emphasized, "to hear her at the time." Exasperated, she reminded Nikki, "Your internal clock is ticking, you know."

How did they get back here? "I know, Mom. And I

promise, when the alarm goes off, I'll get you a grand-child even if I have to steal one."

"Wonderful—my daughter, the felon."

"Everyone has to have something to look forward to," Nikki said cheerfully. The bell went off. Slipping her hands into oven mitts, she took the casserole out and brought it back to the table. She set it down in front of her mother, then took her seat. "So, what's new in your life?" Nikki asked, spooning out some of the stew on to her plate.

"You mean other than a disrespectful daughter?"

"That's not new, that's old," Nikki reminded her mother and then smiled as the meal hit bottom and flavor radiated out. "Hey, this is good, Mom," she enthused. "I've forgotten how much I like your stew."

Maizie perked up. "I'll cook for you every night when you're married."

There'd been times when her mother's persistence got under her skin and annoyed her. But it had gotten so familiar, it now had the aura of home about it.

Nikki laughed, shaking her head. "Thanks, but I can go back to takeout. Besides, I'm too busy for a hus-band." After several disastrous choices, she had resigned herself to being alone. "No man is going to want to compete with a thriving practice."

"Your patients will outgrow you," her mother pointed out. "They'll move on." The implication was clear. She would be alone again.

"New ones'll come," Nikki said.

"And they'll outgrow you, too." Maizie placed her

hand on top of Nikki's, cornering her attention. "Play your cards right and your own children will never outgrow you, Nikki."

"They will if I nag them," Nikki said pointedly.

Maizie drew herself up. "This isn't nagging. This is suggesting."

Nikki grinned. "Over and over and *over* again."

Maizie nodded her head. "Just until the suggestion is taken, dear."

Nikki quickly put another forkful of stew into her mouth to keep from talking and giving voice to the thought regarding suggestions and where they could be put that streaked across her mind.

Whenever anyone talked about which sign they were born under in the zodiac, Maizie always maintained that she was born under the sign of The Optimist. And she had good reason to feel that way. With the notable exception of losing her husband years before she should have, life seemed to just go her way. The day after she'd had dinner with Nikki, life ushered the perfect prospect for her daughter into the real-estate office she ran.

That was when the first client of the day walked through her door. Beyond a doubt, the tall, muscular, dark-haired stranger with the face of an action hero had to be the best-looking man she'd ever seen outside of a movie screen. Maybe even *on* the screen as well. His name was Lucas Wingate and it turned out that he was new to the area. The man was looking for a house for himself and his seven-month-old daughter. Not only was he looking, but he actually bought one.

To add icing to the cake, once he'd made up his mind about the house, he'd said, since he was new to the area, could she possibly recommend a pediatrician for his daughter.

Maizie thought she'd died and gone to heaven. Since Nikki's last name was Connors and Maizie used her maiden name at the agency, she'd sung praises about her daughter without telling him the connection. When he asked if she had sold "Dr. Connors" her house, she'd slyly sidestepped the question by saying she'd put a roof over Dr. Connors's head.

And then crossed her fingers.

Funny how you got accustomed to things without even realizing it, Lucas thought several days later as he glanced around the waiting room.

Take coming to the doctor. He no longer felt like a fish out of water whenever he walked into a pediatrician's office, despite the fact that more likely than not, he was the only male over the age of ten in the room. He'd long since become used to the curious looks, covert and blatant, that would come his way from the other adult occupants of the waiting room.

That wasn't about to change any time soon, he thought. It just no longer bothered him. He'd been Heather's mother and father from the time she was seventy-two hours old. That meant taking on duties he'd never in his wildest dreams thought he'd come within ten feet of tackling. He'd certainly never thought about this less than emotionally satisfying side of parenting when Carole had called him from the doctor's office with the news, so excited that she was utterly incoherent.

Eventually, he got her to calm down long enough so that her words were no longer colliding into one another, forming gibberish rather than making sense. Between Carole's gasps and her squeals of joy, he quickly realized that his wife of two years, the light of his life, was telling him that he was eight months away from becoming a father.

It seemed like a million years ago, he suddenly thought. Damn, he wasn't supposed to go there, wasn't supposed to dwell on what couldn't be changed.

With effort, he refocused.

Now that finding a suitable house was behind him and Heather and his days at the hotel were numbered, Lucas decided there was no time like the present to take Heather to meet her new pediatrician. He wanted the doctor to be acquainted with his daughter before any sort of an emergency arose. He couldn't think of anything worse than having a first meeting in the middle of the night in the emergency room.

These days, Lucas believed in being methodical, in being organized and having all his bases covered. He was a far cry from the carefree computer programmer he'd been a short seven months ago. Becoming a father and losing a wife, going from supreme joy to agonizing sorrow, all in the scope of seventy-two hours, changed the way a man looked at everything in life.

Trying to hold on to his squirming daughter while filling out the forms that the nurse/receptionist had handed him turned out to be more of a challenge than Lucas had initially thought. His handwriting, never good under ideal conditions, looked as if he'd dipped a chicken in ink and allowed it to race across the pages several times over.

It probably made the doctor's handwriting look legible, he thought.

"Sorry about that," he apologized when he finally returned the forms and the clipboard to the receptionist.

Lisa glanced down at the top form, then looked up at Lucas and his restless daughter. She flashed a sunny smile at him. "You did a lot better than most of the people filling out forms while trying to hold on to their little bundles of energy." She clipped the forms inside a brand new, flat pink folder and inserted the folder behind the others standing at attention on her desk. "Take a seat," she directed, nodding at the chair he'd just vacated. "There's a small wait."

The receptionist's definition of "small" definitely differed from his, Lucas thought as he tried his best to amuse a more than slightly cranky Heather. In this case, "small" turned out to be another fifty minutes. Technically, given that he was his own boss and did most of his work at home, his hours were as flexible as he was and he could spare the time. At least, he could today. And Maizie Sommers *had* said that this pediatrician was one of the best in the area.

"Mister Wingate?"

Thank God, Lucas thought, hearing the deep, rumbling male voice uttering his name.

Looking toward the opened door that led to the doctor's exam rooms, Lucas saw that the voice belonged to a slightly balding man of medium height and medium build. A man who, he thought, could have easily escaped notice as he mingled with the rest of humanity. He didn't look as if a voice that deep could belong to him.

"Here," Lucas said eagerly in case the man didn't see him standing up. "Let's get this show on the road, Heather," he murmured.

Crossing the toy-laden, child-filled waiting room, Lucas quickly strode over to the man in the white lab coat who was holding Heather's pink folder.

"Doctor Connors?" Lucas asked when he reached the man.

The latter laughed, shaking his head. "Afraid not. I'm Bob Allen, Dr. Connors's head nurse."

"Oh." He supposed it was a natural mistake. He wasn't accustomed to male nurses. Lucas hoped that the man didn't take offense at his surprise.

Following Bob through the winding hallway and making a left turn, he was aware of several closed doors. Heather's old pediatrician had only two rooms plus his own office. "Are all these exam rooms?" he asked.

Bob looked over his shoulder and Lucas thought he detected a hint of pride in the man's thin face. "She's extremely popular."

"She?" Lucas echoed. Surprise number two. He'd just assumed, since Heather's previous pediatrician had been a man and no pronoun was used in reference to the present one—even the name on the door only had a first initial—that Dr. Connors was a man. Obviously, he'd assumed wrong. "Dr. Connors is a woman?"

"Last we checked," Bob responded with an amused chuckle. "Now, let's get acquainted with the young lady, shall we?" he said, looking at Heather.

In response, Heather picked that moment to let out a frustrated wail.

"Well, her lungs are fully developed," Bob noted as he opened the pink folder.

Skimming down the pages, he asked questions whenever he felt something needed clearing up or if what the baby's father had written down was incomplete. Bob made a few notations in the margins, nodding to himself. Finished, he closed the folder and held it against his shallow chest.

"Well, that about does it on my end. Dr. Connors'll be right in," he promised just before he left the room, closing the door behind him.

Lucas heard Heather's folder being tucked into the slot that had been mounted on the door just for this express purpose.

"Won't be long now, Heather," he told his daughter.

Heather scrunched up her face anyway, making known her displeasure at having to wait. "You and me both, kid," he murmured under his breath.

It occurred to Lucas, some twenty minutes later, that none of the people who worked for Dr. Connors had any kind of concept of time. Granted, he didn't have to be anywhere in particular this time, but in the future, he would be on a tighter schedule, depending on what software project he found himself working on. Didn't this woman have any regard for other people's time?

Lucas found himself growing more annoyed by the moment.

He couldn't afford to waste the better part of his day waiting for a pediatrician to put in an appearance, no matter how good she supposedly was. There had to be *someone* equally as good, or at least almost as good, who knew how to show up on time.

He heard the door open behind him. So much for making good their escape, he thought. But he wasn't about to stand quietly by, agreeing to having his time wasted by virtue of his silence.

Prepared to give this Dr. Connors a dressing down, Lucas turned around to look at the doctor his daughter more than likely *wouldn't* be seeing in the future.

Anything he was about to say evaporated from his tongue and simultaneously vanished from his mind without leaving so much as a single trace.

This *couldn't* be the doctor. She was too young, not

to mention much too striking. The woman had blond hair the color of sunshine on an early spring morning and eyes like a bright, cloudless sky. If anything, with those cheekbones, she belonged on the cover of a fashion magazine. This had to be another nurse, he thought. Just how long did they expect him to wait?

"I'm afraid I'm going to have to—"

"Leave?" the slender blonde in the lab coat guessed. "I'm really sorry about the delay, but if you can spare a few more minutes, I promise to be thorough *and* fast."

That's when it hit him. "You're Dr. Connors?" Lucas asked skeptically.

The bright smile that flashed had more wattage than the lamp on his nightstand. "Guilty as charged. I realize that I must have given you a terrible first impression," she apologized again, "but it really couldn't be helped. One of my patients decided that her bath towel had magic properties. Full of the kind of confidence found only in eight-year-olds, she tied it around her neck and tried to fly off the top of her brother's bunk bed. Needless to say, the towel wasn't magical. Ally wouldn't let Dr. Gorman—the pediatric surgeon—touch her unless I was in the room with her."

Her apology tendered, the woman's attention shifted to Heather who had stopped fussing so much and appeared to be listening to the sound of her voice. Dr. Connors smiled at Heather. "And who is this beautiful young lady?"

Heather gurgled in response, as if to answer her.

Chapter Two

Lucas watched his daughter in muted awe.

The only other person the tiny light of his life had ever responded to in a positive manner was his father. That had struck him as unusual at the time because, brusque, deep-voiced and accustomed to storming his way through life, Mike Wingate was the living embodiment of his former profession—that of a Navy SEAL.

When it came to the rest of the world, Heather was either shy or tearful. So when she appeared to be listening to the doctor's voice instead of fussing or trying to bury her face in his shoulder, Lucas had to admit he was both surprised and impressed.

"She seems to like you."

"Most kids do, unless I've got a needle in my hands," she deadpanned. "I need to get her undressed for her exam," Nikki told him.

He opened the snaps at the bottom of Heather's romper. "At the risk of sounding like a stereotypical father," he told his daughter's new doctor, "Heather isn't like most kids." To prove it, he added, "She doesn't like *anybody* except for me and for my father."

Nikki undid the diaper tabs, first on one side, then the other, leaving the diaper in place for the moment. "That must really be hard on her mother's ego," she commented, working her fingers gently along Heather's nicely rounded tummy.

The image of Carole, lying in the hospital bed, Heather pressed to her breast, flashed across his mind. "I imagine that if she were around, Heather would be different."

Her new patient's parents were obviously not together, Nikki concluded. She wondered if the divorce had been acrimonious. Babies sensed and reacted to so much more than people realized.

She made her voice sound nonjudgmental as she asked, "You don't have joint custody?"

"No."

She wouldn't have said that the word had exactly been bitten off, but it definitely had the ring of finality. Huge "no trespassing" signs were popping up all around the subject.

As she resealed the diaper tabs, Nikki silently admitted that her curiosity had been aroused a little. But she wasn't attempting to satisfy her curiosity when she pressed Heather's father for more of an explanation. She needed a full history on the child. This included finding out just what kind of living conditions her patient had to deal with on a daily basis. Doing without any contact with her mother could have some far-reaching consequences down the line.

"Do you need me to do anything else?" he asked, wanting to make this examination as painless as possible for his little girl. He still couldn't believe she wasn't fussing.

"I can take it from here, Mr. Wingate," Nikki answered, slowly edging him away from the examination table with her body. "Okay, let's see what makes you tick, little one."

Watching her little patient carefully, Nikki began going through the rest of the paces for a routine exam. She checked Heather's reflexes as well as her response to different stimuli. She checked her overall skin tone and, in general, looked over anything that would enable her to have a clearer picture of as many aspects of Heather's health as possible.

Using a small rubber hammer, she gently struck just above each sturdy knee. The response was immediate. "Strong kick," Nikki commented with approval. "I'd say she was a good candidate for martial-arts training in a few years. Everything going well at home in regards to her care?" she asked casually as she continued her examination. "No questions, no concerns?"

Lucas sighed. Most of the time he felt like a lost tourist in a foreign country who didn't speak the language. "A thousand questions and concerns," he heard himself saying.

Not a day went by when he didn't question his ability to handle this latest twist life had thrown him. Granted, he'd gotten better at some things, but he was far from confident.

"Well, I don't know about a *thousand* questions, but we can get started with a few," she told him, "and I'll do my best to answer them." She took out another instrument. Switching on the light, she looked inside Heather's ears. Heather made a noise that was clearly a protest. "I know, I know," she said soothingly, switching to the other ear, "it's no fun having someone stick things in your ears. I'll be quick," she promised, then lowered the instrument. "See?" she said to the baby. "All done."

"You talk to her as if she's able to understand," Lucas observed. He talked to Heather himself, but it was just to fill the silence. He didn't really believe she understood him.

Nikki turned her head and looked at him over her shoulder. A tolerant smile curved the corners of her mouth.

"Never underestimate these little beings, Mr. Wingate. They have razor-sharp minds and are capable of absorbing things like multi-surfaced sponges." Nikki stopped talking long enough to listen to Heather's chest. All clear, she noted happily. Nothing was more beautiful than a healthy baby, she thought. "You can get her dressed now," she told Heather's father.

Picking up Heather's folder, she made a few notations, then glanced over the top sheet Wingate had filled out. The handwriting, she observed, left a lot to be desired. It took her several seconds to make sense of the words. It wasn't easy.

"I see that Heather's current with all her immunizations." Nikki raised her eyes to look at him. Finished with dressing his daughter, the man now held Heather against him. "That your doing?"

At times, the responsibility for this newly minted human being still overwhelmed him, but he was doing the best that he could. "Yes."

Nikki nodded, closing the folder again. "Commendable."

Lucas lifted his shoulder in a careless response, brushing off the compliment. While he was still struggling to hit some kind of rhythm when it came to raising Heather, he hadn't thought of what he was doing as being anything outstanding or even out of the ordinary. It all had to do with keeping his daughter healthy and thriving. Heather was the reason for his existence. She was what kept him going. If he lost her, there'd be no reason for him to breathe anymore. It was as simple as that.

As a question occurred to her, Nikki opened the folder again and glanced over the personal information page, zeroing in on the line requesting the name of Wingate's employer.

"You work at home?"

He nodded. "Most of the time." He'd been self-employed for several years now. "I own my own business." Which was a fortunate turn of events. "It makes being with Heather easier."

Nikki nodded absently. Closing the folder, she held it against her chest as she studied the interaction between father and daughter for a moment. There was definitely a bond, she thought. Most first-time fathers of infants usually held them as if the slightest wrong move would cause the infants to break. Heather's father held his daughter as if he'd had a great deal of practice at it. Nikki couldn't help wondering how long he'd been on his own and why.

Had his wife walked out on him? Had having a baby been his idea, not hers? If so, had he talked his wife into it, only to have her balk at the responsibility, at being tied down once the baby was born?

In Nikki's opinion, these were questions that needed some kind of answers. At least cursory ones. But there was no easy way to broach the subject.

She'd watched Wingate as he'd dressed his daughter. There was a great deal of love evident in the simple act. She'd been at this for a while and Wingate didn't act like a parent who felt as if he'd been saddled with a heavy burden.

Nikki decided to proceed cautiously.

"So, is Heather's mother completely out of her life?" She tried to make the question sound casual, but had a feeling that she didn't quite manage to pull it off. Especially when Heather's father looked up at her sharply.

"Why would you want to know something like that?" Lucas asked her.

Nikki heard the wariness in his voice. She also felt as if she was being challenged. "This is supposed to be a complete history and physical."

"Of the baby," he retorted tersely.

The parting had definitely *not* been on the best of terms, she thought.

"Yes," she answered evenly. "And Heather's background is part of what contributes to her makeup. Most of the babies I see are brought in by their mothers. Occasionally, both parents come in. But very rarely do I see a baby brought in only by his or her father. There is the exception," she allowed, then went on to illustrate it. "Mom's sick so a slightly out-of-his-element Dad takes over and brings the infant in. And, every now and then, there is the househusband. But we've already established that that's not you." She opened the folder again, but this time, she didn't need to read it. She'd already gleaned what she needed to know. "Everywhere it asks for information on Heather's mother, you've left the space blank."

"I know," he replied, his face devoid of any kind of expression.

The omissions had been deliberate. After seven months, it was still too painful to go into anything dealing with Carole, too painful to even write down her name. He was trying his very best to move on, to seal himself off from yesterday and only live in today while keeping his eyes focused on reaching tomorrow.

But he wasn't quite there yet and bringing up memories of Carole would only impede any progress he might be making or even hoped to make.

"Be careful, Mr. Wingate," Nikki cautioned quietly.

"Careful?" he repeated. What was the woman talking about? "Careful with what?"

"Animosity has a way of spilling out and contaminating anything it comes in contact with."

Is that what she thought was happening? "You mean Heather?"

She gently ran her hand over the baby's downy head. Heather gurgled. "That's why we're both in this room, isn't it?"

"There is no animosity, Dr. Connors," he told her, his voice tight. "There's just pain."

He hadn't admitted that, not even to himself. What was he doing, baring his soul to someone he didn't even know?

She had patients waiting for her and the waiting room, she knew, was filled. But she couldn't just walk away from the pain she saw in Lucas Wingate's eyes.

She placed a comforting hand on his shoulder. "Whatever happened between the two of you, you have to forgive her. For Heather's sake as well as for your own. I know it might not be easy, but—"

"How do I forgive her, Doctor?" The words were forming and coming out against his better judgment. It was almost as if he couldn't stop them. "How do I forgive Carole for dying?"

Nikki's eyes widened. "Excuse me?"

"My wife," he said, "how do I forgive her for dying and leaving me like this? This wasn't the way it was supposed to have been. I wasn't supposed to do this alone."

It took Nikki a second to recover and a couple more to catch her breath. Talk about being blindsided. "Your wife is dead?"

The very word skewered into his gut like a jagged corkscrew. Lucas struggled not to let his emotions overpower him and come rushing out. He could feel his hands forming angry fists even as he held Heather. Fists that had nothing to hit.

His voice was monotone as he replied, "Yes."

Nikki felt almost ghoulish for probing, but she needed to ask. This was for the record—and to get her to understand Heather's father a little better. "How did it happen?"

He looked at her sharply. "What does it matter?" Lucas demanded.

"It matters," she assured him, her eyes shifting to Heather, her implication clear.

All right, he thought. Maybe the doctor was right. Maybe it was necessary for Heather's records. If that was the case, he might as well get this out of the way and not put it off any longer.

"Carole died seventy-two hours after giving birth to Heather. The doctor said it was some kind of complication due to childbirth. She suddenly started hemorrhaging in the middle of the night." He tried not to see it in his mind's eye, but it was hard not to. "It all happened so fast, they didn't have enough time to save her. I woke up when the nurse who'd come in to check on her hit code blue and all sorts of medical personnel started running into the room." There was no place he could hide from the anguish that snared him. "My wife was dying and I was just sleeping through it."

He was obviously a loving husband, otherwise he wouldn't have been sleeping in his wife's hospital room. The man was being too hard on himself. "You couldn't have known."

His eyes were blue flames. "I should have," he insisted angrily. "Carole and I were in tune to one another. We finished each other's sentences. I should have sensed what was happening." His voice came dangerously close to cracking. "She was gone before I could say goodbye."

What was it like to have someone love you so much? Nikki wondered.

Her last relationship, short-term though it had been, had ended when her boyfriend told her to stop wearing her heart on her sleeve. He found it embarrassing. But she was who she was. Ever since she could remember, she had always been compassionate. It was, Nikki firmly believed, what made her a good doctor.

So, moved by Wingate's story and more so by the pain she heard in his voice and saw in his eyes, she didn't hesitate. Sharing in his grief, Nikki hugged him. The moment she did, she felt him stiffening.

Most likely embarrassed by his own display of emotion and her response to it, the man had sealed himself off, she thought. Nikki took a step back, letting him restore his space.

"Have you told anyone this?" she asked.

"I just did."

And he was more than just a little annoyed with himself for doing it. The strain he was under was bigger than he thought. This wasn't like him. He didn't just go around spilling his guts like that. He knew better than that.

"No," she said gently, "I mean to someone professional."

He wasn't following. "You're not a doctor?" he asked, confused. "I thought—"

Taking pity on him, Nikki spelled it out for the man. "I was referring to a psychologist or at least a grief counselor."

He had no desire to sit in a room and relive the ordeal with a stranger. Once was way more than enough for him.

"I was raised to work things out on my own," he told her.

He was resurrecting his walls, Nikki thought. She could hear the distance in his voice.

"Sometimes that doesn't always work out. There's nothing wrong in asking for help. Everyone does it at one point or another," she assured him. Her words, she could tell, were falling on deaf ears.

"I'll keep that in mind." His tone said just the opposite.

Nikki retreated. There was no sense in pushing, she told herself. Lucas Wingate was here for his daughter, not to be badgered no matter how well-intentioned she might be in her suggestions.

Turning toward Heather who had kept amazingly quiet during this whole exchange, she smiled at the round little face. With her curly light blond hair and bright, blue eyes, Heather was nothing if not adorably huggable. The girl's mother had to have been fair-haired, Nikki caught herself musing, since the man standing before her fell into the tall, dark and handsome category, with brown hair so dark it almost looked black. And his eyes were almost a navy blue, unlike the shining blue stars that Heather had.

"Well, the good news is that you've been doing everything right. Your little girl seems to be the picture of health and thriving very nicely. Whatever you're doing, keep doing it," she advised cheerfully.

"Mostly I've been stumbling around in the dark," he admitted. Maybe Carole was looking down on them, keeping their daughter safe. "I never gave parenting much thought until now," he admitted. It was more like trial by fire than anything else. The last seven months had seemed more like seven years. "When does it start getting easier?"

As far as Nikki had gleaned from her practice, it didn't. "I'm told that the first fifty years are the hardest."

"Fifty?" Lucas echoed incredulously.

She laughed at the stunned expression on his face.

"At least, that's what my mother maintains." She glanced down at the folder she was still holding, remembering something she'd glossed over earlier. He'd moved here from the east coast just a short while ago. "Do you know anyone here yet?"

Lucas shook his head. "Haven't had the chance to really talk to anyone yet. Heather and I just moved to the area three weeks ago." He'd tried to make a go of staying where he and Carole had lived, but everywhere he turned, he'd been there with Carole. Everything he saw reminded him of Carole. He couldn't move on. Even just breathing was hard. So, he'd moved. "I thought we could do with a fresh start."

Translation—he was running from memories. The downside of loving someone with your whole heart, she supposed. Either way, Heather's father was new here and, as of yet, had no one to turn to. That wasn't good.

Without realizing it, Nikki caught her bottom lip between her teeth, working it as she did a quick tally of pros and cons in her head. The "cons" far outnumbered the "pros" but she felt sorry for Wingate and that one thing tipped the scales drastically in his favor. She made her decision.

Taking one of her business cards out of her oversize pocket, Nikki did something she'd never done before. She wrote her cell phone number and home number on the back of the card, then held it out to him.

He looked at her quizzically.

"Seeing as how you're new here and really new at all

this," she nodded at Heather, "I thought you might like to have something to fall back on."

Taking the business card from her, Lucas looked at the numbers she'd just written on the back. Her handwriting, he couldn't help but notice, was even and utterly legible.

So much for stereotypes. "Are these the numbers for the hospital?"

"No, that's my cell number. And that one is my private number." His quizzical expression deepened. "The middle of the night is a scary time to have no one to turn to," she explained. "The middle of the night is also the time that most children under the age of seven pick to get sick. If Heather suddenly comes down with something and you find yourself in a bad way, call me."

He stared at the card for a moment and then at her. "You don't mind?"

Nikki laughed. "If I minded getting calls in the middle of the night, I've spent an awful lot of years studying to get into the wrong profession. Don't worry," she assured him, "I'm used to it. After office hours, parents call my service and then my service calls me." She indicated the card he was still holding. "I just got rid of the middle man for you." Her smile was one of warmth and compassion. "No one should have to do this alone for the first time. You need a support system in place, at least until you're ready to take off the training wheels."

A knock on the door interrupted anything further she

had to say. Bob popped his head in. "Mrs. McGuire's Teddy is getting very restless."

So what else was new? "On my way," she assured the nurse breezily. She spared Lucas one last look. "You're doing just fine—both of you."

And then she was gone.

Chapter Three

Weary, Nikki walked into her house and dropped both her purse and her keys on the antique table—a house-warming gift from her mother—beside the door. The keys fell off, landing on the travertine floor. She left them there. If they'd nicked the tile, so be it. She didn't have the energy to care.

She'd just begun to kick off her shoes when the landline rang.

Nikki didn't bother suppressing the groan that rose in response.

Please let that be some telemarketer on the other end wanting to sell me something or find out how I feel about the spring TV lineup. Anything, just not another emergency. I'm not up to it tonight.

After her office hours were over, Nikki had gone across the street to Blair Memorial. She had several pint-sized patients who'd been admitted in the last few days and she felt she couldn't very well call it a night until she checked on them before going home.

August Elridge's parents had cornered her for a full half hour, taking turns shooting questions at her. It was clear to Nikki that they were both bona fide hypochondriacs. The eight-year-old had been admitted for a routine tonsillectomy. Less than twelve hours after surgery, he seemed to be doing very well.

Too bad the same couldn't be said for his parents.

Approaching the ringing phone on the wall landline as cautiously as if she were trying to get closer to an angry anaconda, Nikki peered at the caller ID.

It was her mother.

Was that better or worse than being called in for an emergency? It all depended, she supposed, on why her mother was calling. She really wasn't up to being on the receiving end of another installment of *Mother and the Unmarried Daughter.*

But she knew her mother. If she didn't pick up before her answering machine came on, her mother would just call her back again.

And again.

Drawing in a deep breath, Nikki removed the portable receiver from its cradle, pressed Talk and placed it against her ear as she headed for the sofa. Might as well be comfortable for this.

"Hi, Mom. What's up?" she asked in the most cheerful voice she could muster. Her energy petered out by the fourth word.

"Nothing," Maizie responded in the same cheerful voice. "I just wanted to touch base with my favorite daughter."

Nikki sat down and put her feet up on the coffee table. She was definitely too young to feel so drained.

"Mom," she tactfully reminded the woman on the other end of the call, "I am your only daughter."

"If there had been more, you still would have been my favorite," her mother blissfully assured her. "Challenging," Maizie allowed, "but definitely my favorite."

There was no point in continuing the debate. Her mother liked to have the last word. Nikki knew when to withdraw. "Well, thank you."

Maizie's mother antennae immediately went up. Nikki sounded as worn out as a sponge that had been pressed into service for over six months.

She was calling to subtly prod and find out if that handsome young widower had been to her daughter's office yet. It had been several weeks since she'd given him Nikki's number. That was a long time by her standards. She'd refrained from calling for as long as she humanly could. If she waited any longer, trying to keep herself contained, Maizie was certain she would rupture something vital inside.

Inadvertently, Nikki had given her her opening. "You sound tired, dear. How was your day?"

On the way home, Nikki had been contemplating soaking in a hot tub but wondered now if that was really such a good idea. In her present state, she just might fall asleep and drown.

Her mother had picked up on that. She might have known that she would. Her mother had hearing like a bat. As for her "intuition," that was usually off the charts. "Good ear, Mom. As for my day, it was hectic."

That was definitely nothing new. Nikki was always running around, doing the work of three people without taking a break. Maizie'd given up chiding her daughter and pointing out that she risked burning herself out. The warnings all fell on deaf ears.

"You always say that, Nikki," she reminded her daughter.

"Okay," Nikki conceded. "*More* hectic than usual. And before you can ask—" she was very versed in the way her mother's mind worked "—on a scale of one to ten, today was a thirteen."

Maizie sighed. Nikki couldn't continue at this pace indefinitely. Eventually, something had to give. "You need to take in a partner."

They'd danced this dance before, too, Nikki thought wearily. According to her mother, her father had worked himself to death and she knew that her mother was afraid that the same fate awaited her, as well. She couldn't exactly fault her mother for loving her or for worrying about her.

Besides, it wouldn't work. Her mother didn't know *how* to stop worrying.

So, rather than argue with her, Nikki just laughed, albeit wearily, and teased, "What, and share all the glory?"

Maizie struggled to refrain from lecturing. That would defeat the purpose of the call. But sometimes, the girl got her so angry… She was just as stubborn as her Justin had been.

"No," Maizie agreed, "but with any luck, you might get a little downtime out of it. You remember downtime, don't you, Nikki? In case you've forgotten, that's when you rest."

"I'm fine, Mom. Really." Nikki did her best to sound upbeat and ready for more rather than someone who'd been summarily run over by a steamroller. Twice. "I like my pace."

Ordinarily, she did. It was when she felt she was doing triple time that it got old.

"I'm sure you do. That way, you have an excuse for not having a personal life."

Maizie bit her tongue the moment the words tumbled out. So much for her silent promise to herself not to alienate Nikki. Maybe Nikki wouldn't take it that way. The next moment, her daughter's reply killed that hope.

"Guess you found me out, Mom. Don't know how the FBI manages to get along without you."

"I don't love the FBI," Maizie answered, her tone serious. "I love you."

Nikki felt like a snippy, ungrateful daughter. Her mother had given up a lot for her to be where she was today. The least she could do was put up with her mother's quirks.

"I know you do, Mom." She blew out a breath. "Sorry, I didn't mean to sound sarcastic. Like I said, it's been an extralong day."

"That's what you get for being so good at what you do. Your loyal, pleased patients wind up recommending you to their friends and your practice winds up growing faster and faster."

It certainly felt that way at times. Her mother's assessment made her think of Heather Wingate and her father. A warm feeling came out of nowhere, spreading over her like a soft, comfortable blanket.

To make up for sounding waspish, Nikki decided to share a moment out of days with her mother. "As a matter of fact, I did get a new patient the other day."

"Oh?" Did that sound as artificial as she thought it did? Maizie wondered. She dialed it down a bit before prodding further. "Anything interesting? Boy? Girl? Twins?"

"It was a girl. Seven months old. Her name was Heather and she was adorable." *As was her father.* Where had that come from? Nikki upbraided herself.

"Would her parents be looking for a bigger house?" Maizie asked innocently. "I could always use new clients and referrals," she added. "You could try to work my name into the conversation—"

"I thought you said business was good," Nikki reminded her.

"It is, but you know this business. You're only as good as your latest sale. It's always hustle, hustle, hustle."

Nikki fondly smiled. When it came to selling, her mother was a powerhouse.

"Sorry to disappoint you, Mom, but I think buying a new house has already been resolved. And for the record, it's not a husband and wife. Heather's father is a single dad."

"Huh," she heard her mother utter the word thoughtfully. "Don't see many of those around. Cute?" Maizie asked.

"The baby's very cute," Nikki teased, knowing full well that wasn't what her mother was asking.

This time, the sound Nikki heard was a little exasperated. "I meant the baby's father, Nikki."

"I know what you meant, Mom, and yes, if you really need to know, he's very cute. And very serious. And—" more importantly to her "—he's also very much in love with his wife."

"But she's—" Maizie had almost said "dead" but stopped herself just in time "—not around," she substituted. "That's not healthy."

That wasn't for her to say either way. "He's not my patient, his daughter is."

Maizie frowned. She had led this horse to water and she was damn well going to see that it drank. "Aren't you the one who's always saying that everything in a child's background contributes to that child's welfare and what he or she becomes?"

"Yes," Nikki admitted unwillingly. And then she shook her head. "How is it that you can always find a way to twist my words around to suit your goals?"

Protestations of innocence would be a waste of time here, Maizie thought. So, instead, she answered, "Practice." And then, for emphasis, Maizie repeated with feeling, "Practice, practice, practice."

Nikki laughed. "I get it. You practice." Nikki stifled a yawn. "Look, Mom, if you don't mind, I'm going to have to cut this call short. Otherwise, you're liable to wind up talking in my sleep."

Maizie took no offense. If she knew her daughter, Nikki had gotten less than five hours sleep, five being the girl's all-time high since she'd graduated middle school.

But still, Maizie couldn't resist asking, "Are you telling me I'm boring?"

"No, I'm telling you that I'm dead on my feet and all I want to do right now is just crawl into bed while I still have some strength left."

"It's not even nine o'clock," Maizie protested. Life was passing Nikki by without making a pit stop. She couldn't allow that to go on. "I'm the one who should be going to bed early, not you—not unless there's someone in that bed to crawl in next to."

Nikki could hear the wide, wicked smile in her mother's voice.

Good old Mom, she never stops pitching.

"If there was a man in my bed, I'd be sure to send him to you. You're obviously the one here with the kind of energy needed to deal with that."

Maizie sighed. "I worry about you, Nicole." In response, she heard snoring noises on the other end of the line. For the time being, Maizie surrendered. At least Lucas had brought his daughter to Nikki. She was just going to have to be patient. "All right, I can take a hint, Nikki."

Nikki laughed. "No, you can't, but I love you anyway. Talk to you soon, Mom."

And with that, Nikki hung up before her mother had a chance to say anything else. You had to be quick around Maizie Sommers, Nikki thought with a fond, if very weary smile.

Still seated, Nikki thought about eating dinner for exactly three seconds, then decided that she'd probably fall asleep waiting for the microwave-oven bell to go off. Besides, she was too tired to chew.

The prospect of going up the stairs was also daunting. So instead, she made her way to the guest bedroom at the back of the house. Discarded clothing marked her path as she stripped off one item after another. She was down to her underwear by the time she reached the room.

Not bothering to turn on the light, Nikki wrapped herself up in the light blue comforter that was on the bed, lay down and was asleep in less than a minute and a half.

* * *

She was surrounded by phones. Big phones, little phones, cell phones, all ringing shrilly and demanding her attention.

The ringing grew louder and louder, until it all merged into one excruciatingly annoying ring that undulated through her body, hurting her teeth.

It's a dream, just a dream.

Struggling to hold on to sleep, Nikki kept telling herself it was a dream—until she finally realized that it wasn't.

The phone on the nightstand was ringing.

She drew in a long, deep breath, trying to clear her head. The bedroom was completely swaddled in darkness. She had no idea what time it was.

The phone rang again. Her brain was having trouble engaging.

Maybe it was the fire department, calling to tell her to evacuate. This was the middle of fire season, which ran inordinately long in Southern California, and although she'd never had to evacuate herself, everyone in this area of the state knew someone who'd been forced to evacuate at one time or another.

That kind of an emergency, dire though it could be, only required her to put one foot in front of the other. She didn't need to be sharp and at the top of her game.

The phone stopped ringing just as she reached for it.

Good, Nikki thought, falling back on to her pillow. With any luck, she could get back to—

The phone began to ring again.

Okay, whoever it was wasn't going away. Fully awake and alert by now, she lifted the receiver and placed it to her ear. "Dr. Connors."

"Doctor, I'm really sorry to bother you at this hour, but you said to call if I had an emergency."

The voice, distressed and breathless, sounded vaguely familiar, but she couldn't quite place it. And how had he gotten her private number? The answering service wouldn't have given it out.

Who had she…?

And then a light went off over her head. She'd given him her phone numbers, cell *and* landline. The widower with the cute little girl.

"Mr. Wingate?" Sitting up, Nikki didn't wait for his acknowledgment. "What's wrong?"

He realized that he hadn't even identified himself when she picked up. The woman probably thought he was an idiot. He was usually more in control than this, but he was rattled, *really* rattled. All that mattered was Heather.

"Heather's burning up."

Nikki kicked her way out of the self-styled cocoon and turned on the lamp on the nightstand. "Define 'burning up.'"

"Hot." There was exasperation, anger and helplessness all wrapped up in the single word.

"What is her temperature?" Nikki enunciated each word slowly and carefully. The man hadn't struck her as one of those inept fathers so badly portrayed in the grade B sitcoms that littered the airwaves. Why was he behaving like one?

"I didn't take it." Lucas barely kept from snapping out the sentence. Getting hold of himself, he explained his inaction. "I was afraid that the thermometer was going to break off in her, um." At a loss, he threw up his hands and said, "She keeps wiggling and screaming. I can't get her to lie still. But her head's really, really hot."

The little girl had seemed fine during her exam the other day, but then, under the age of seven, children's temperatures could be all over the map. High in the morning, normal in the afternoon and spiking again in the evening. It was enough to drive fear into the hearts of first-time parents.

"When did this start?" she asked.

Where were her clothes? Nikki looked around the room and then remembered her unintentional striptease as she made her way to the guest room earlier.

Getting up, she began to retrace her steps. Piece by piece, she reassembled her outfit as she made her way to the front of the house.

Lucas closed his eyes and tried to remember when he'd first noticed that Heather's forehead was hot. "About three hours ago." Guilt sliced through him as he recalled, "I thought I was imagining things and I put her to bed. But Heather kept crying and she just kept getting hotter and hotter. I don't know what to do for her," he confessed. "Should I bring Heather to the emergency room at the hospital?"

Blair Memorial was an excellent hospital, but even its staff could only go so fast in a crowded E.R. Heather needed to be seen as soon as possible—before her father became a patient, too.

"No, why don't you let me take a look at her first," she suggested. Because he was self-employed, she knew he had a private, individual plan as far as medical insurance went. Private plans usually didn't even come close to covering basic visits. "There's no need to have you waiting in the emergency room—or paying for it—if you don't have to."

She was in the living room now, the discarded clothes collected and bunched up against her. Nikki deposited them on the sofa. "Why don't you give me your address and I'll come over to see if Heather actually needs to go to the hospital. Most likely, all she'll need are some antibiotics."

"You make house calls?" he marveled.

"I make exceptions," Nikki corrected. And this was a judgment call. Opening a drawer in the kitchen, she fished out a pen, then saw that she was out of paper. Improvising, she pulled off a sheet from the paper-towel rack and placed it on the counter. "Okay, give me your address."

There was a long pause. Still not used to his new address, Lucas had to think before he could answer her. After a beat, he recited his phone number, as well.

"In case you have trouble finding the house," he explained.

Nikki smiled to herself. She'd grown up in this city, watching it evolve from a two-traffic-light town to a thriving city of ninety-thousand-plus people. Because of her mother's chosen profession, she was familiar with every residential development Bedford had to offer.

"I'll be there as soon as I can," she promised. About to hang up, she stopped and put the receiver back to her ear. "Hang in there, Mr. Wingate. Heather's going to be all right."

There was a time when he would have balked at her thinking that he needed reassurance. But having to raise Heather on his own had changed all that. He needed help and he knew it. Pride wasn't allowed to get in the way. There was far too much riding on this.

His voice was almost rigid as he said, "I know. It's just that—"

He was afraid of losing the little girl, Nikki thought. She deliberately kept her voice calm, soothing. "You don't have to say it, Mr. Wingate. I understand. I'll see you in a few minutes."

She ended the call and crossed back to the living room. Dropping the portable telephone on the sofa, she hurried into her clothes. The phrase, "No rest for the weary" kept echoing over and over again in her head.

Truer words were never written, Nikki thought with a sigh. She kept a fully packed medical bag in the hall closet in case an emergency arose.

This, she thought as she quickly checked the contents to be sure she had what she needed, qualified as an emergency.

At least, she knew, it definitely did in Lucas Wingate's eyes.

Chapter Four

Lucas Wingate had bought a house in one of Bedford's newer developments, Nikki noted as she drove to the address he had given her. Upon entering the upscale residential development, she had to admit that she was impressed.

While the developments within Bedford began to multiply, spreading out to both ends of the city and eating into what was once sprawling farmland, the size of the lots the houses stood on kept decreasing. Land was most definitely at a premium. This particular development, she recalled her mother telling her—whimsically dubbed Camelot by the developer—had yards that rivaled the size of the original developments, now some thirty-eight years old.

Big yards in *Camelot* translated to big price tags.

Obviously, Mr. Wingate was doing quite well for himself, Nikki mused as she pulled up in front of the two-story Tudor-styled house. Maybe she needn't have been all that concerned about his ability to handle the kind of expense that a trip to the E.R. usually generated.

Still, volunteering to see Heather at his house was really the best way to go, she decided. Going to the E.R. with a wailing baby was only marginally easier than walking barefoot across a mile of broken glass. There was no way of knowing how many people would be waiting in the E.R. by the time Wingate arrived.

Sometimes, miraculously, a patient could be in and out in under an hour, but more than likely, several hours would have to pass before tests could be taken and a diagnosis arrived at. In the meantime, Heather would continue crying and Wingate would become more and more anxious about his daughter's health.

This was definitely better.

As she walked up the blue-gray stone-paved path to the front door, she could hear the sound of a baby crying in heart-wrenching distress. The closer she came to the house, the louder the crying grew. By the time Nikki reached the door, it sounded as if Heather was right on the other side, wailing her little heart out.

Lucas was probably a basket case by now, Nikki guessed.

Shifting her medical bag to her other hand, Nikki rang the doorbell. The door immediately sprang open, as if it was wired to instantly respond to the sound of the door chimes.

An ashen-faced Lucas, barefooted with his shirt unbuttoned and hanging open and his dark hair tousled as if he'd combed it with a fork, stood in the doorway. Nikki couldn't help thinking that despite his distress, he looked rather sexy, rumpled. Heather, crying for all she was worth, was propped on his left hip. He was subtly rocking her, but the normally soothing motion seemed to have no effect on his daughter.

Nikki was surprised that he could even hear the doorbell with all this noise.

The relief she saw on Lucas's face was almost palpable. He looked at her as if he expected her to perform a miracle.

"You got here quickly." Lucas practically shouted to be heard above Heather's wails. He backed up and opened the door farther.

Crossing the threshold, Nikki raised her voice and said, "I don't live that far away." Putting her bag down, she gently took Heather from him. "Let's have a look at the patient." Tears slid down Heather's chubby cheeks but her wails went down half a notch as the baby looked at her curiously.

Heather was waiting for a miracle, too, Nikki thought, feeling for the anguish the baby was experiencing.

The wails started up again in earnest, stronger than

before. "I know, honey, I know. You hurt. But we're going to make you feel all better. I promise." Raising her eyes to Lucas, she asked, "Where can I examine her?"

"Her room's upstairs, but you can use the sofa." He gestured toward it.

There was a pink blanket, half on the floor, half draped over the cushions, hiding most of the soft, navy leather sofa from view. From what Nikki could see, it was a finely crafted piece of furniture but its importance, like everything else in the very cluttered room, had fallen by the wayside, taking a backseat to his sick daughter's needs.

Glancing swiftly around at the surroundings, Nikki took it all in. The living room looked like a tornado had hit it. There was no reason to believe that the clutter was isolated to one room.

Either Lucas hadn't yet gotten the hang of being a father, or ministering to a sick baby had completely undone him. Most likely, it was a little bit of both, topped off with the burdensome fact that the man was still trying to deal with the cross-country move and settling into his new home. Sealed boxes stamped with a moving company's logo were shoved into various corners.

"Sofa it is," Nikki agreed.

But when she went to deposit Heather on to the blanket, Nikki bit back a gasp. Heather had managed to grab fistfuls of her hair, holding on for dear life. The pain went shooting across Nikki's scalp.

Very carefully, Nikki coaxed the baby's hands open,

detangling herself from Heather in order to put the little girl down on the sofa. It wasn't easy.

"C'mon, Heather, let go of the doctor," Lucas urged, managing to help loosen the baby's grip.

Finally free, Nikki commented, "You weren't kidding about her being hot." Just holding the baby against her had allowed the extreme difference in body temperature to register.

The anguish in Lucas's eyes intensified. "Should I call 911 for an ambulance?" By the time the question was out of his mouth, he was halfway across the room, reaching for the telephone.

But Nikki raised her hand to stop him. "We're not there yet." Not wanting to shout over the baby's cries, she beckoned Lucas over to the sofa. "Watch her for a minute for me." They traded places and he sat down, using his body to barricade Heather on the sofa. "Where can I wash my hands?" Nikki asked.

"Kitchen's right over there." Lucas pointed to the doorway on the left.

"Be right back," she promised. Her words were addressed to the baby.

More clutter met her when Nikki walked into the kitchen. Dishes were piled up in the sink, empty boxes of take-out food overflowing the steel garbage container. It looked as if the man hadn't had a moment to himself since he'd moved in.

She washed her hands and used one of the last sheets from the paper-towel rack to dry them. Returning to the living room, Nikki reclaimed her place on the sofa beside the baby.

"If you could bring my medical bag to me," she told Lucas as she sat down, "I'll get started."

The request caught Lucas off guard. He looked around the room, at a loss. "Where…?"

The man really was tired, Nikki thought, amused. But even worn-out, he still looked damn good. With his shirt hanging open like that, she could see that there were ridges where most men had the beginning of a gut. Somewhere along the line, he had to have found time to work out. Either that, or he was just very blessed.

"It's right by the door." She pointed to where she'd dropped the bag.

The expression on his face said he vaguely remembered that she'd come in with it. "Oh, right." Lucas fetched the navy blue bag and hurried back with it. A rueful smile came and went from his lips as he held it out to her. "Sorry, I'm not usually so scattered."

Her smile was warm and reassuring as she glanced up at him. "It takes a bit to get the hang of it. Nobody's born knowing how to be a parent and unfortunately, babies don't come with instruction manuals. Even if they did," she laughed softly, "it would all change the second they popped out."

Opening the bag, she took out a pair of rubber gloves and pulled them on. Nikki debated for a moment between using a strip thermometer and going with the more accurate rectal kind. She opted for the strip. No point in making the baby even more uncomfortable, she thought. She could make allowances for the point difference.

Lucas stared at what looked like a strip of colored paper. "What's that?"

"It's a different kind of thermometer," she told him. "Noninvasive."

He regarded the rectangular strip dubiously. "Is it any good?" And then, laughing shortly, he dismissed his own question. "Of course it has to be good. You wouldn't be using it if it wasn't." Trying to see what had registered on the strip, Lucas stood beside her and leaned in to read what number had been reached. The angle made it difficult to make out. "What does it say?" he asked.

Despite the situation, Nikki realized how aware she was of Lucas standing next to her, as close as a breath, with his shirt just hanging open, an impressive physique for the viewing.

But, just like with the overly cluttered living area, she managed to block it out.

Removing the strip from Heather's forehead, she raised her eyes from the thermometer to Lucas's face. "It says 'take a deep breath, Mr. Wingate,'" she deadpanned.

For a second, Lucas looked at his daughter's doctor, confused. And then he got it—and felt like an idiot. "Oh, you're kidding."

"Obviously not very successfully," she conceded. Looking at the strip, she announced the numbers. "It's 103 point seven."

"103 point seven," he echoed, his throat all but

closing up on him. His eyes darted toward Nikki's face. How could she be taking that in so calmly? Lucas tried not to panic, but he barely succeeded. "Shouldn't we be putting Heather into a tub filled with cool water or something?"

"If it starts to climb higher or doesn't break in an hour or so, yes, we could do that. But only if it's absolutely necessary."

He bit his tongue to keep from saying that he thought it was necessary *now*.

As Lucas watched, the doctor methodically and swiftly checked Heather's ears, her nose and her throat, all under the most vehement protests, the type that could have jarred all the teeth of an enraged bull.

Listening to Heather's chest was a particularly tricky feat. Nikki got an earful, mostly of the baby's loud cries. Nikki felt as if her head began to vibrate. Removing the stethoscope, she dropped it into her medical bag.

Finished with her quick exam, Nikki came to what she felt was an appropriate conclusion. Not one to draw things out for a dramatic effect, she asked Heather's father matter-of-factly, "Have you noticed Heather drooling the last few days?"

Since Heather had come into his life, Lucas found himself going through a lot more shirts than he used to. Several of them had been so heavily stained, they had to be thrown away.

"She always drools," he told the pediatrician with a dry laugh.

Nikki rephrased her question. "Have you noticed her drooling a lot more in the last few days, then?"

About to say no, Lucas stopped and thought for a minute. Unsettled by her exam, Heather was crying even louder than before and it was difficult for him to concentrate. When he finally managed to, he suddenly remembered.

"Now that you mention it, yes, I have. Why?" His eyes widened warily as fear reappeared, darker and bolder than before. "What does it mean? What does Heather have?"

Nikki noticed Lucas was holding his breath. He was obviously afraid of what she was about to tell him. Now that she'd made her diagnosis, the first order of business was to calm him down. Quickly.

"Nothing dangerous," she assured the man with feeling. "From all indications, Heather is cutting her first tooth."

"A tooth?" he repeated incredulously. All this fuss over a tooth? It just didn't seem possible. "Isn't Heather a little too young for that?"

"Not at all. Most babies get their first tooth sometime between four months and seven months, although some are even older and occasionally, the rare baby is born with teeth. When that happens, they usually have to pull them."

It didn't make sense to Lucas.

"Why?"

"Several reasons, actually," she told him. "Babies wind up biting their tongues, sinking their teeth into their lips, things like that. It's safer for the baby—and the poor mom if she's nursing—if they're toothless for the first few months of their lives."

He glanced down at his daughter, who was sniffling and appeared to be gearing up for another round of wailing. Just how many tears were in that little body? Why hadn't she worn herself out yet? Heather had certainly worn him out.

"So, this is what the fever and the crying is all about?" he asked Nikki. "Teeth?"

"Tooth," Nikki corrected. "Just one. But it hurts like anything. The tooth is struggling to erupt through the gum. That makes her gum extremely sore." She smiled at him. "But I've got something for that."

"You do?"

She hadn't thought that it was possible to cram in so much relief and joy into two words. "Yes, and you can get it in any pharmacy, but I usually have some available in my medical bag—just in case." She noticed just a touch of sorrow in his expression as Lucas regarded his daughter. "Face it, Daddy. It was bound to happen. Your little girl is growing up."

Nikki reached into the medical bag and took out a small bottle filled with an amber liquid. Putting a little on the tip of her finger, she gently inserted her finger into the baby's mouth and then rubbed the solution along her gums, both upper and lower for good measure.

Heather momentarily closed her gums over her finger, biting down. After a few moments, the baby's tears stopped flowing. Nikki carefully removed her finger from the girl's mouth.

She drew in a long, cleansing breath and then released it. Her finger was throbbing. "She's got good jaws, I'll give her that," Nikki quipped.

"And that's it?" Lucas asked. "She's going to be better?"

"To be on the safe side, I'm going to give Heather a shot of Tylenol to lower her fever, but for the most part, that should do it. You'll need to rub more of this on her gums in the morning. And you might want to give her a teething ring as well. Keep it in the freezer until you give it to her. The cold'll soothe her gums as she chews on it."

Lucas seemed a little confused. Nikki read his expression correctly. "You don't have a teething ring, do you?"

Lucas raised his shoulders in a helpless shrug. "I didn't think she was going to need one for at least another few months."

She thought as much. "Lucky for you, I have one of those, too." Rummaging through the medical bag, Nikki found a teething ring, still in its original package, and took it out.

"Here, take it out of the package and put it into the freezer for the time being. You're going to need it later."

He took the ring from her. "You certainly do come prepared," he marveled.

"That comes with practice," she told him with a smile. "After a while, you learn."

He had his doubts about that though as he went into

the kitchen to put the teething ring into his freezer. Just as he walked back into the living room a couple of minutes later, Heather let out another wail.

He immediately stiffened, braced for something new. "What?"

"Like most little people, your daughter doesn't like getting shots," Nikki told him as she put a cap back on the needle she'd just used. There was a small container in the bottom of her bag where she inserted used needles to keep them apart from the rest of her things.

Slowly, Heather's fussing abated. Lucas ran a hand over his daughter's downy head. The way he felt about the child, despite his exhausted expression, was evident in his eyes.

"I don't know how to thank you, Dr. Connors." Reaching into his back pocket, Lucas took out his wallet. "How much do I owe you? Because, whatever it is, it isn't enough."

Picking the baby up, Nikki began to rock her slowly and pat her back. Heather had already stopped wailing and had finally settled down. *Won't be long now,* Nikki silently promised, then turned to look at the baby's father.

"We'll talk about that later," Nikki told him. She studied him for a moment, although she really didn't need that much time to come to a conclusion. The man was dead on his feet. "When was the last time you slept, Mr. Wingate?"

"I'm not sure." He took in a long breath. Man, he was tired. "What day of the week is it?"

"That's what I thought. Why don't you get some rest?" she suggested. He began to protest, but she cut him off. "I'll stay here and monitor Heather for a little while, make sure there's nothing else going on."

Lucas looked at the woman who had just done the equivalent of walking on water as far as he was concerned. He was torn between a desire to take her up on her offer and knowing that her offer went far beyond anything he had a right to ask.

Making up his mind, he shook his head. "No, I can't ask you to do that."

"You're not asking," Nikki pointed out. "I offered." Before he could turn her down again, she added, "If I'd wanted to avoid calls in the middle of the night and everything that came with them, I would have become a skin doctor, not a pediatrician. Now please, stop arguing and get a little sleep—you've already wasted at least three minutes arguing."

He didn't have the energy to argue. And, he reasoned, Heather couldn't be in better hands right now. If he didn't get some sleep soon, he would wind up being a danger to not just himself, but to Heather as well.

"Okay, you win. I'll just close my eyes for a few seconds. That's all I need," he told her, sinking down into a recliner.

She continued swaying, holding Heather against her chest. The baby was definitely falling asleep. She kept her voice low. "You'll feel better in bed."

"I'll feel guiltier in bed," Lucas countered, his eyes

closing just as his daughter's had. "This way," he continued, his voice growing softer, his words more spread apart, "if Heather starts to fuss again, I'll be right here to take over."

She was about to answer, but then she stopped. Holding the dozing Heather against her and still patting the baby's back gently, Nikki drew closer to Lucas in order to get a better look.

And then she smiled to herself. Just as she thought. The man was out like a light.

"You've really been giving your Daddy a hard time, haven't you, Heather?" she asked softly, moving away from the recliner and the sleeping man. "You're going to have to lighten up on him a little, sweetheart, or he's going to wear out before you're a teenager and the *real* fun begins."

The baby curled into her, her small head nestled against her neck. All sorts of warm, liquid feelings spread out through her limbs.

Nikki sighed.

"You're right, Mom," she murmured quietly under her breath. "I'd really love to have one of these of my own. But there's not much chance of that happening anytime soon, unless I wanted to go the test-tube route—and that wouldn't be fair to the baby. So, as long as I keep picking men who leave something to be desired in the relationship department—like participation—you don't get to be a grandmother."

Nikki sighed, remembering the last few dating disasters, including Larry, the ob-gyn. "None of them would have made a decent father." She glanced over toward Lucas, who was now definitely asleep. "Not like this guy. You're a lucky little girl," she said to Heather. "You know that? A very lucky little girl."

Nikki took in a deep breath. There was no use in rehashing the past. Except to learn from it. The one thing she had learned was that some people just weren't meant to get married.

In this case, that meant her.

Chapter Five

Lucas didn't remember falling asleep. Moreover, he didn't know exactly what it was that finally woke him up. What he did know was that, for once, it wasn't his daughter's crying.

It wasn't any sort of noise at all.

If anything, his dream had startled him into wakefulness. Even that was strange. Ever since Carole had died, he hadn't dreamt at all. But this time around, inexplicably, he had.

He dreamt that he, along with someone whom he recognized as his best friend, were doing their best to negotiate their way through an active minefield. The farther into the field he went, the harder his heart pounded.

And then there was an explosion.

His "best friend's" luck had abruptly run out and he'd stepped on a mine. The misstep had cost the man his life.

Sweating, his heart pounding hard enough to all but crack a rib, Lucas awoke with a start.

And immediately thought he was still asleep.

Taking in a deep breath, Lucas tried desperately to rouse himself, to pry open his eyes and banish the last remnants of the sleep-laden fog from his brain.

But his eyes wouldn't open—because they already *were* open.

This *had* to be a dream. Otherwise, why wasn't he hearing Heather? Where *was* Heather?

For that matter, where was his clutter?

There were no newspapers piled on the coffee table, no brigade of unopened, economy-size packages of disposable diapers standing against the wall in one corner of the room. No empty baby bottles scattered about on any and every flat surface, waiting to be gathered up and washed.

Lucas looked around incredulously. Everything was neat and tidy. He'd all but forgotten a living space could be like this. It reminded him of the world he'd once known, before Heather had come into it. The world he'd known when Carole was still alive. Granted, he'd never been a great one for cleaning up after himself, but things had never hit critical mass until he'd become a single father.

Lucas still wasn't hearing her. Where was his daughter?

"Heather?" he called out, pulling himself out of the

recliner, a maneuver the rest of his body vehemently protested. The sleep he'd gotten represented the first un-interrupted rest he'd had since the move.

Feeling a sense of panic spreading out from the center of his chest, Lucas hurried into the next room, the kitchen, and then stopped dead. The sink no longer had pots and dirty dishes overflowing. The box of pretzels that had comprised his dinner were no longer on the counter. Neither were yesterday's empty jars that had contained baby food. Or was that today's?

What the hell was going on here?

This wasn't a dream, it was the beginning of a night-mare.

His daughter was missing.

And then the thousand and one pieces free-floating in his head pulled themselves together, slowly forming bits and pieces of a whole. The doctor had come here, he recalled. Had the woman decided to take Heather to the hospital? That would explain his daughter's absence, but not why everything was suddenly so neat and tidy. It was as if he'd been whisked away to an alternate universe.

He didn't want a neat house, he wanted his daughter. "Heather!" he called out louder.

"If she actually answers you, my mother knows this publicist who can get you bookings on cable channels and the late-night talk shows. You can bill her as the Amazing Heather."

He swung around to see that Heather's doctor had come up behind him. Without Heather.

"Where is she?" he asked, doing his best not to sound as anxious as he felt.

"Heather's in her room." He really was a good father, wasn't he? she thought. "I just finished checking on her. She's sleeping like the proverbial baby." Nikki smiled at him. He looked a little bewildered. Poor man, this was really hard on him. "So were you."

Lucas dragged a hand through his unruly hair. Embarrassed, he asked, "How long was I out?"

Nikki glanced at her watch. It was getting close to 1:00 a.m. He'd been out like a light for the last two hours. "Not long enough. In my opinion, you could do with a little more sleep."

He tried to shake off the last of the sleepiness that still clung to him. He didn't like feeling disoriented. Or in debt. "How long have you been here?"

"The entire time," she answered simply.

Lucas shook his head. He wasn't making himself clear. "I mean in hours."

"A couple or three." It was closer to three, but there was no point in nitpicking.

"A couple or three?" Lucas echoed incredulously. How was that possible? He'd just sat down in the recliner for a minute. But he had to have been asleep close to at least a couple, he reasoned, looking around. It would have taken at least that much time to have cleaned up— unless the doctor had dibs on a magic wand.

"Well, at least there's nothing wrong with your hearing," Nikki quipped.

Lucas scanned the area around him again, half expecting the neatness to morph back into the clutter he'd made his peace with.

"And you did all this?" He swept his hand around the area.

"No, the shoemaker's elves did," she deadpanned. "When they came in and found that you didn't have any shoes that needed fixing, they decided to clear up the clutter instead. They've got a strong, stern union to answer to."

He stared at her. The doctors he was used to roller-skated in and out of an exam room, even the one who had informed him that Carole would no longer be part of his mornings and nights had been detached, brusque and quick. None of them would have *ever* made a house call, much less cleaned that house.

"Why?"

"Why have they got a union?" Nikki guessed at his question. "I don't really know. You'll have to take it up with them."

"No, why did you do this? Why did you clean up?" He realized he didn't know if her effort had stopped with the kitchen, or if she'd continued cleaning everything in her path. Guilt sank in deeper.

Nikki lifted a shoulder in a careless half shrug. "Nervous energy," she told him. "Heather was asleep and I'm not very good at sitting still."

She didn't bother adding that she'd never met a mess she couldn't conquer and that she had a weakness for restoring order. Surface disorder was the easiest kind to work with, even chaotic disorder like what she'd found in Wingate's house.

"You could have gone home," Lucas pointed out.

"I said I'd watch Heather for you, remember?"

He hadn't meant to encroach on her time this way. She'd already done far more than he'd expected by coming here to treat his daughter.

"Why didn't you wake me up?" he asked.

"I believe that would have come under the heading of cruel and unusual punishment," she told him. He looked so adorably disheveled, she had to fight back the urge to push his hair out of his eyes. "A man in a coma would look like he was on a double dose of Ritalin compared to you."

He didn't understand the reference. "I thought Ritalin was supposed to calm you down."

"That's the way it works on children," she clarified. "On adults, it has the exact opposite effect. Turns you into that mechanical rabbit that can go on forever without recharging."

"I guess I was kind of dead on my feet," Lucas conceded.

"Kind of?" Nikki laughed at the mild term he used. "Mr. Wingate, I looked out the window. There were vultures circling the house."

He had to admit that he felt a great deal more human now than he had in a week. "How do I thank you?"

Nikki inclined her head, a warm smile on her lips. "You just did."

There was something in her smile. Something that got under his skin. Despite what he'd said, Lucas found himself reluctant to have her just leave. Reluctant not because having Heather's pediatrician here created a sense of security for him, or because she was a natural beauty, even under less than perfect circumstances, but because she seemed to understand what he was going through. And that meant a great deal.

Lucas hated to admit it, even silently, because it negated the image that he'd had of himself, but he needed this act of kindness, needed it in order to feel part of the human race again.

"If you do this for everyone, when do you have time for yourself?" he asked.

"I don't do this for everyone," she told him truthfully. "Only for those parents who look as if they're about to float out to sea on an eight-by-ten ice floe." Her voice was soft, calming. "You're new here, and by your own admission, alone. I felt that you needed a helping hand."

There was no arguing with that. "A helping hand, a helping foot, a helping body in between," he agreed, nodding his head.

If he felt that way, she could do something else for him. "Well, if that's the case, I could get you a list of nannies— all excellent—who you might consider hiring—"

But Lucas stopped her. He couldn't do it, couldn't palm his daughter off on someone else. "My wife would have never wanted me to hire a stranger to raise our daughter," he protested.

She'd never met a father who wanted to do it all. Usually, the idea of a nanny was something they grasped on to with both hands, thankful that there was a light at the end of the tunnel and that they could make a break for it without guilt.

"Part-time, then. Someone to relieve you once in a while, or for a few hours each day. Maybe every other day. However you want to work it." She made her strongest argument for considering the idea. "Just so that you don't lose sight of who you are."

Or thought she did. But his reply both negated her approach and also raised him up another notch in her estimation.

"I know who I am," Lucas insisted. "I'm Heather's father."

Still, he needed to step back and look at the whole picture, take the future into consideration, not just this tiny part. "As she gets older, Heather's going to want you to have more credentials than that. You can't build your life around one person because that person is going to feel caged if you do. And when they burst out of that cage, *you're* going to feel abandoned. Not to mention that you'll find yourself in the middle of an identity crisis." Which was why so many stay-at-home mothers suddenly found themselves at a loss as to what to do when their "babies" grew up and became adults, she thought.

He watched her for a long moment. She was afraid maybe she'd offended him—and then he laughed. "Wow, minister to sick babies, vanquish clutter with a sweep of your hand, all while handing out indispensable advice. Is there anything you can't do?"

"Bending steel with my bare hands comes to mind," she quipped. "Other than that—" Nikki spread her hands out wide and gave a little careless shrug. "I'll let you know."

"Can I make you a cup of coffee?" The offer came out of the blue.

"If you really want to do something for me, get in bed." It was only after the words were out that Nikki realized what they must have sounded like to Heather's father. Like an invitation. Embarrassed, Nikki tried to backtrack. "I meant—"

Was it his imagination, or were her cheeks turning a light shade of pink? The least he could do was spare her any embarrassment. Lucas held up his hand, quickly stopping any need for an explanation.

"I know what you meant."

But even as he assured her that he understood her suggestion was absolutely innocent, a little seed came out of nowhere, a seed that took her words and let his imagination run in a pleasant direction.

"But," he continued as if the image of her body next to his wasn't taking on a life of its own, "I think having a cup of coffee with someone who single-handedly put my life back on the right track trumps getting a few more minutes of shut-eye."

Amused, and definitely up for coffee despite the hour, Nikki pointed out, "You might regret surrendering that time if Heather wakes up in a few minutes."

"I'm one of those guys who can make do on next to no sleep," he confided, really starting to come around. "It was the absence of that 'next to' that was starting to do me in. Thanks to you, I'm good to go for at least another forty-eight hours. *Really,* thanks to you," he emphasized, taking another look around as he led the way into the kitchen. "How did you know where every-thing went?" he asked her as he took an opened coffee can out of the refrigerator and placed it beside the baby monitor on the counter.

"I've got an innate sense of where everything goes." Nikki took a seat at the table. "My mother's a real-estate agent. When I was a little girl, she used to take me with her whenever she conducted an open house on the weekend. When anyone arrived, she'd take them on a guided tour. I'd entertain myself by taking my own tour. I'd explore cupboards and closets and bureau drawers."

Lucas measured out two servings of coffee, deposit-ing the granules into the coffee filter. Then he poured two cups of water into the coffeemaker and hit the brew button. The machine instantly made gurgling noises as it heated the water and routed it over the granules.

"In other words," he summarized with a grin, "you snooped."

"Research," Nikki corrected, pretending to be serious. "I conducted research into the human condition."

Lucas took out two mugs from the cupboard overhead. "I'd say that was a very lofty term for snooping."

"Yeah," Nikki conceded. "But that's how I know, more or less, where things generally go."

"Well, you did a great job. The place looks a hundred times better than it did when Heather and I moved in. It was starting to look really hellish around here."

"You know, if you don't like the idea of a nanny, you might want to consider a maid service," Nikki suggested. "Have someone come by once a week, once a month—how long have you been in this house?" she asked suddenly, interrupting herself.

His back to her, he poured the coffee into the two mugs. "A little more than a month."

"Once a week might be better," she decided. Unattended, housework had a tendency to multiply geometrically. "That way, you don't have to take away any time from your daughter to fight your way through the clutter and straighten up."

"Not a bad idea." He glanced at her over his shoulder. The woman seemed to be on top of everything. "I suppose you have a list of available cleaning women, too." It was more of a statement than a question.

One day every two weeks, Nikki closed her office and donated her time at a free clinic, providing care for the babies of women—in some cases, girls who had barely reached puberty—who couldn't afford to bring them to a doctor. Several of the women were looking for jobs. They were willing to take on any honest work because they had no special marketable skills.

"As a matter of fact," she replied, "I can give you the names of a couple or three."

"Who you could personally recommend?" he asked. He owned state-of-the-art computers, as well as equipment that helped him develop the software he marketed. He needed someone he could trust coming into his house, not someone he would have to watch. That defeated the whole purpose of hiring help.

"As people, yes," she said without hesitation. "But as far as the caliber of their work goes, I can only assume that they'd do an excellent job. I haven't had the occasion to need their services myself."

Lucas brought over the two ten-ounce mugs and placed one in front of her. Backtracking, he took a container of flavored coffee creamer and put that next to her mug.

"Why would you if you cleaned like this at home?" He saw no reason to go through the expense. "Sugar?"

She shook her head. "This sweetens it enough," she answered, picking up the creamer. She added a drop, then two, then more to the inky darkness, until she was satisfied. The coffee was now the color of extralight chocolate. And the creamer container felt a good deal lighter. "Sorry," she apologized. "I didn't mean to take so much."

"After what you just did, you could have taken a cow and it wouldn't have been too much—not that I don't intend to pay you, I do. Whatever it comes to is fine with me."

Nikki shook her head in silent disapproval. "Never agree to something unless you know the bottom line ahead of time," she warned him seriously. "My father taught me that one."

Lucas took a long sip of his coffee. That, too, made him feel a little more human. And awake. "Sounds like a smart man."

A fond, sad smile steeped in nostalgia curved her lips. "He was."

Lucas focused on the single crucial word. "Was?" he asked.

She nodded. Both hands wrapped around the mug, she took another sip and waited for it to wind through her system, warming it. "My father died just before I turned twelve. That's one of the reasons why my mother went to work full-time as a real-estate agent. "

"Oh." It hadn't occurred to him to ask about that. He was a product of the times. He'd grown up with women being part of the workforce without needing to give excuses or justify their reasons for working. Even Carole, who'd wanted nothing more than to be a mother, had thought about returning to work when their baby was old enough.

Life was going to be perfect. Everything had been mapped out, he thought sadly. Except they hadn't factored in the unpredictability of life and its tendency to throw those curveballs when least expected.

But they weren't talking about him, they were talking about Heather's doctor, he reminded himself.

"I'm sorry for your loss." And then he paused. "That doesn't begin to cover it, does it?" he asked. He put himself in her position. "The words, they don't seem like nearly enough."

"Oh, I don't know. At times, 'loss' has a depth and breadth that seems as if it doesn't have an end in sight. But life goes on, especially if you have a child." She took one last sip, draining her mug and setting it down on the counter again. "My mother said I always kept her centered, even through the worst of times."

She pushed back her chair and rose. He was quick to get to his own feet. "Well, thanks for the coffee, but if I'm going to be any good to anyone tomorrow—" Nikki glanced at her watch and amended "—today, I'd better get going."

Lucas walked her to the door. She'd come here a stranger, but in these last few hours, she'd become so much more than that. He felt as if they'd spent half an eternity together. And that they'd connected during that time.

"I don't know what I would have done without you," he told her quite honestly.

At the door, she turned around to face him. "Survived, Mr. Wingate. You would have survived," she assured him.

"Lucas," he prompted.

Nikki cocked her head. "Excuse me?"

"You came to my daughter's rescue and saved my sanity. I think that entitles you to call me by my first name."

"All right, Lucas," she allowed. "Bring Heather in on Thursday. Call Lisa for an appointment and tell her I want her to fit you in. We'll see how that tooth of hers is behaving."

Nodding, he opened the door for her, then watched as she walked back to her car. He didn't feel nearly as lost as he had a few hours ago. Things were falling into place, his daughter was asleep and he had someone to turn to.

Lucas took none of that for granted.

Chapter Six

"So, how's our girl doing?" Nikki asked, addressing the question to the little girl propped up on the table as she walked into exam room two.

Heather's folder was in her hand, but she hadn't opened it yet. Instead, she relied on what she saw—a very happy, healthy-looking baby—and what the baby's father would tell her. If there was something wrong— or not completely right yet—Wingate would fill her in within the first three minutes.

He appeared as happy as his daughter and a great deal more rested than when she'd last seen him two days ago.

"You were right," Lucas told her. "She was cutting a tooth."

Taking the baby's chin gently into her hand, Nikki coaxed her mouth open.

"And there it is, tiny and white and right in the middle of her lower gum," she declared, pleased. The worst was behind Heather—until the next tooth.

Heather closed her mouth down on her finger. The baby was still teething, Nikki noted. There would be another tooth coming in soon. She'd left Lucas enough gum medication to see him through several teeth. He was going to need it.

"No more fever?" she asked him, gently removing her trapped finger.

"No more fever," he confirmed, guarding the wiggling baby to keep her from making a dive for the floor. Heather was a study in perpetual motion. "She's been her happy self again these last two days."

"Terrific," Nikki said, pleased.

She made a notation in the folder, then closed it again. Leaving the folder where it was for the moment, she smoothed down the frilly pink dress the baby wore. Her father was dressing her as if she were sugar and spice, but underneath that, Nikki had a feeling that Heather might have a tomboy streak in her.

Good for you.

She smoothed down the dress's hem. "Have you looked into getting a nanny or a housekeeper yet?" she asked Lucas.

"I thought I'd hold off until I saw you," he told her. "I'd rather go with a recommendation than just take a shot in the dark and call a number out of the classified pages in the phonebook."

"Always a good idea," Nikki agreed. And then a question occurred to her. "Is that how you came to me? Did someone recommend me to you?"

Lucas picked Heather up and tucked her on to his hip. Heather settled in as if she belonged there. "As a matter of fact, yes." And he would be eternally grateful to that real-estate agent, Lucas thought.

It was the one line that Lisa had accidentally forgotten to include when she'd printed up the new forms, the line that asked if the new patient had been referred by someone. Nikki liked to stay on top of that.

"If you don't mind my asking, who was it who referred you?"

"It was—"

But before Lucas had a chance to tell her, there was a quick knock on the door and then it immediately opened. Bob stuck his head in. "Sorry to interrupt, Doctor," the nurse apologized, "but Mrs. Henderson just called. Ptolemy did it again."

Nikki sighed as she momentarily closed her eyes. The woman definitely needed to watch her son more carefully. "What did he use this time?"

Bob grinned, obviously entertained by the boy's antics. "She thinks it was one of his brother's miniature figures."

"He's getting to be very creative," Nikki commented dryly. "Tell her to bring him in. I'll take him as soon as she gets here."

"You got it." Bob closed the door.

She could feel Lucas looking at her curiously before she even turned around to face him. "Mrs. Henderson's youngest likes to stick things up his nose. Frequently."

He laughed shortly. "I would too if my mother named me Ptolemy."

"She has a penchant for unusual names. She named her other sons Cicero and Euripides."

This Henderson woman definitely had a problem, he thought. "I hope they're being homeschooled—or that she's at least taking them to martial arts classes." Otherwise, he had a feeling they were being picked on daily—or worse.

"As a matter of fact, they are being homeschooled," she told him. "But I think you might be on to something with the martial arts classes. They're going to need them when they get older. Can't hide in the house forever." For now, her own curiosity had to be put on hold. Not that it was a burning question. Heather's father was probably referred by the mother or father of one of her patients. Most likely, he lived near one of them. "Well—"

Again she was interrupted by a knock on the exam room's door. Bob was back.

"Almost forgot to tell you, Dr. C, the computer tech guy called. Said he wasn't going to be able to fit you in until sometime late next week. With luck."

"Terrific." This time, rather than triumphant, the single word had a world of weariness wrapped around it and tied up with a bow.

"Hey, I'm just the messenger," Bob informed her before withdrawing and closing the door behind him.

As with all things that had to do with the computer, Lucas's interest had been stirred. "Your office computer have a problem?" he asked.

"No, thank God, or I'd really be in trouble." Heather, she noticed, was drooling again. Taking a tissue from the dispenser, she wiped the baby's chin. Lucas had another rough night in his near future. "It's my home computer," she said, tossing the tissue into the waste-paper basket. "It's been acting up for a month now. I'm beginning to think it's possessed. It arbitrarily shuts itself down whenever it wants to. Whole sections of data disappear. Sometimes they come back when I re-boot, sometimes they don't. I really don't know what to do to get it back to its old self."

She was referring to the computer in human terms, the way he sometimes did. Lucas found that amusing. "I can take a look at it for you."

"I couldn't ask you to do that."

Lucas raised his eyebrows. "Said the woman who came over in the middle of the night to hold my hand and take care of my sick baby."

"It wasn't the middle of the night," she recalled. "I just happened to collapse early on Tuesday."

"Late or not, you still went out of your way," he reminded her. "Computers are my thing. It's what I do for a living *and* a hobby. Don't make me beg, Doc. Let me help." Satisfied that he'd made his point and glad that he'd found a way to repay her in some small way, he asked, "Is it a laptop?"

It was as large a laptop as she could find at the time. She got it so that she could tuck it away when she entertained. It had been on her dining room table for two years now.

"As a matter of fact, yes, it is."

"Good, I can pick it up from you, either from your house." He realized she might not be comfortable with that, so he suggested additionally, "Or you can bring it in to your office and I'll swing by here to get it."

Nikki didn't mind putting herself out for her patients, or her friends, but she definitely felt uncomfortable about being in debt to anyone who wasn't family or a lifelong friend. Lucas was too busy with his daughter, his new house and his career to be put out like this.

"I'll get back to you on that," she promised.

As Nikki put her hand on the doorknob, about to leave, a third knock reverberated on the other side of the door. This time, it was her receptionist who pushed the door open.

Because of the resistance Lisa felt as she tried to come in, she glanced down on the other side of the door as she pushed it open.

"Oh, I thought it was stuck," she remarked, then got down to the reason she was there. "Mrs. Williams is on line three. She says she needs to talk to you right away."

Mrs. Williams was another one of her regulars. One she could easily do without if the woman ever suddenly decided to uproot her family and move to the opposite coast.

"What is it this time, Lisa?" Nikki asked. "Is Janine talking in tongues or did she master Beethoven's Fifth with one hand tied behind her back?"

Lisa grinned. "I didn't ask. Line three," Lisa repeated.

This time, she didn't even have to turn around to know that Heather's father eyed her curiously. "Mrs. Williams thinks that her four-year-old daughter, Janine, is a gifted prodigy. Since I'm Janine's pediatrician, Mrs. Williams feels compelled to call every time she perceives that her daughter had done something outstanding."

"And does she?"

"She does as far as her mother's concerned. Her main achievement to date was being toilet trained at eighteen months."

"And that's early?" Lucas asked.

She knew what he was thinking. He was measuring his days in diapers being changed. Without thinking, she placed her hand on his shoulder in mute comfort. "I'm afraid so. I'll see you later."

It was a throwaway line, but he heard himself using it as a link. "You really could use some downtime, you know."

"I've got some scheduled for 2012," she assured him, opening the door. "May 4th."

"How about something a little sooner?" he posed. Catching her attention, he continued. "Say like Saturday? I'd like to say thank you by making you dinner," he added quickly, despite the fact that cooking wasn't something he did with any degree of expertise. He had a feeling that if he offered to take her out, it might seem like stepping over the line to her. "Unless you're busy."

It never occurred to Nikki to play games or act coy. "No, I'm not busy. But won't you be?" she asked. "With Heather?" she clarified when he looked at her, somewhat puzzled.

As long as Heather was fed, dry and not crying, he could keep her in her port-a-crib and juggle several things at the same time.

"When she's not sick, I've gotten pretty good at multitasking," he answered. "Besides, my mother taught me that one good turn deserved another. She would have never forgiven me if I took what you did the other night for granted and just walked away."

She already knew that his mother had passed away a long time ago. As much as her mother drove her crazy at times, she knew if she ever lost her mother, the feeling would be unbearable.

"I wouldn't want to offend the memory of your mother," she agreed.

"Good." He knew he only had a few seconds before she was gone. "Saturday," he repeated. "When's a good time for you?"

She thought for a second. There had been things she had been meaning to get to. Nikki left herself a little leeway. "Six?"

"Six," he agreed, nodding. "And bring your laptop with you," he told her. "I'll see if I can arrange an exorcism."

He was referring to the fact that she'd called it possessed, but he wasn't laughing at her or making her feel as if she was a computer dummy. She appreciated that. "That's over and above the call of duty," she told him.

"So's what you did the other evening," Lucas countered.

Nikki had a strong feeling that she wasn't going to win this debate and she had to admit, she rather liked that in a way. Liked someone taking charge.

Other than her mother, of course.

She loved her mother more than anything or anyone in the world, but she really balked when the woman took it upon herself to try to commandeer her life from time to time. She often attempted to steer it in a certain direction, one her mother thought was right for her.

"Okay," Nikki surrendered. "I'll be there at six." Heather made what sounded like a squeal just as Nikki started to walk out of the room. "Yes, I will see you then," she said to the baby as if she were responding to a question. And then she left.

Heather's smile went from ear to ear.

Lucas picked up the all-purpose bag he carried with him whenever he left the house with Heather and slung it over his shoulder before he switched his daughter over to the same side.

"You know, Heather, if I didn't know any better, I'd

say you and the lady doctor were communicating."
Heather raised her eyes up to him and went on smiling.
"Maybe you are at that," he said under his breath.

"Hi, darling."

Maizie did her best to sound cheerful, but she absolutely hated talking to her daughter's answering machine. While it didn't really bother her one way or
another to leave messages on anyone else's machine, it
irritated her when she had to do the same thing on
Nikki's. Not the least of which was because half the
time, her messages went unanswered and unreturned.

"I was wondering if you were up to a dinner and a
movie tomorrow. Chinese and an action movie," she
specified. "I'd rather see that new romantic comedy that
just opened, *Jeannie's Secret Lover*, but I know you
prefer action movies, so we'll go see *Fatal Explosion*
instead. Get back to me when you can." Maizie threw
in a little guilt for good measure. "I'll be the mother
sitting patiently by her phone—"

There was a noise on the other end and Maizie
thought she heard the receiver being picked up.

"Hello, Mother sitting patiently by her phone."

It looked like she'd lucked out after all, Maizie con-
gratulated herself. "Is that really you, Nikki? Or have
you trained your answering machine to be clever?"

"Yes, Mom, it's really me."

There was a breathless note to her daughter's voice.
She'd obviously caught her either coming in, or hurry-

ing off. Either way, she'd take it. "Great. So, how does dinner and a movie sound?"

"It sounds wonderful," Nikki began.

"Good!" Maizie declared, relieved. Because of their busy, conflicting schedules, it had been a while since they'd gone out together and she did enjoy her daughter's company. "Then I'll—"

"But I can't."

Having gotten Nikki live and in person, at least on the phone, Maizie refused to accept defeat so easily. "If you're on call, we can still go out. I'll understand if you have to rush off in the middle. And, most of the time," she added quickly, trying to cut off any protest that might be coming, "they don't even call you."

"I'm not on call this weekend, Mother," Nikki told her patiently.

"Then what's the problem? If you're not on call, then you're free to go out."

If she told her mother the truth, Nikki knew she'd be leaving herself open to intense grilling, both now and right after she came home. Still, she hated the idea of lying to her mother. The very first man she'd ever fallen for lied as effortlessly as he breathed. She absolutely refused to be like that self-centered slimeball.

"I'm sorry, Mom, but I'm busy."

"Busy doing what?"

She could tell her mother's curiosity had really been aroused. "Just busy." Even as she said it, Nikki knew she'd never get away with that. In the name of love, her mother wasn't the type to respect boundaries. At least not hers.

There was silence on the other end of the line and just for a split second, Nikki thought—hoped really—that she was in the clear. But then, in the next second, hope came crashing down and died a fiery death when she heard her mother say, "You've got a date, don't you?"

Maybe if she explained. "It's not a date, Mother," Nikki told her. "It's…dinner."

"With a girlfriend?" Maizie asked in a lofty tone, her voice clearly indicating that she doubted it.

"With someone who is going to fix my laptop." That, at least, was the truth.

"I can think of other things that need fixing first," Maizie murmured under her breath, knowing that it was loud enough for her daughter to hear. "You're going out to dinner with a computer technician?"

Nikki shut her eyes. *Just say okay and hang up, Mom.* "Not exactly."

Maizie gave every indication of digging in for the long haul. "Then what 'exactly?'"

"He's not buying me dinner, Mother, he's making dinner."

"Oh." The single word was bursting at the seams with meaning.

"No 'oh,' Mother. If you must know, it's the widower. The one I mentioned to you the last time," she recalled. "His baby was running a high fever late one evening and he called me in a panic. I came over—"

"You came over?" Maizie repeated. She had trouble containing the feeling of absolute triumph vibrating within her. She did her best, though. "I thought that house calls went the way of the eight-track tape."

"Stop interrupting, Mother," Nikki requested. "I came over, I gave the baby a shot, she got better. He's grateful. End of story."

No, my darling, it's only the beginning. God willing.

"I would imagine he'd be grateful," Maizie agreed. "And he's making you dinner?"

"That's how he wants to show his gratitude," Nikki explained, feeling helpless. Once her mother got hold of something, it was like trying to pull a bone out of a pit bull's mouth. Next to impossible unless a gun was involved.

"I can think of better ways to show gratitude," she heard her mother say.

"He's also going to take a look at my computer," Nikki reminded her. "He's a software programmer or engineer or something."

"Handy man to have around in this day and age." Nikki could *hear* her mother smiling. "So, what's this grateful programmer's name?"

She wasn't stupid. "Oh no, I'm not telling you his name."

"Why?" Maizie asked innocently.

"Because I know better than to give you any more information." She'd already told her mother too much, Nikki thought. Why hadn't she let the answering machine just take the message? It would have been so much easier that way.

"You're exaggerating, Nicole."

So, now they were getting formal. Her mother was playing the mother card. Well, referring to her by her full name no longer had the same effect that it had when she was ten.

"No, Mother, I'm not. I tell you his name and you'll be printing up wedding invitations by Sunday morning."

"Don't be silly, dear," Maizie dismissed the protest. "Sterling's is closed on Sundays," she reminded her daughter, mentioning the printer she'd been bringing her business to for the last ten years. "I'd have to wait until at least Monday."

The awful thing was, her mother was only half kidding. If that much. "How about until Hell freezes over?"

She heard her mother groan in earnest. "Oh, please tell me you'll be married before then, Nicole."

"I'm not having this conversation with you again, Mother." And then she relented. Just a fraction. "What will be will be, remember?" Her mother used to tell her that whenever she would ask about the future as a little girl.

"Yes. It's a nice song by Doris Day. From some classic Hitchcock movie as I remember," Maizie said dismissively. "However—"

"No 'however,' Mom. Oops, there's a call coming in," Nikki announced suddenly. "Gotta go. Love you."

And with that, Nikki terminated the call. There was no other phone call coming in, but she knew her mother wouldn't give up until *she* gave up Lucas's name. And while she'd exaggerated what her mother would do with it, she knew that giving her mother a name would make everything that much more real for the woman. And there was nothing to make "real." It was just dinner with a grateful parent, that was all.

A grateful parent who just might be able to fix her laptop.

Maizie looked at the receiver in her hand and smiled. Broadly.

So far, so good.

She wondered if it was against some basic, ancient rule if she drove down to the Mission at San Juan Capistrano and lit a few candles at the altar tomorrow morning, given that she wasn't Catholic.

Thinking it over for a moment, Maizie decided it wouldn't hurt to cover all bases.

"If you would like to make a call—" the metallic voice emerging out of the receiver began.

"Yes, but you don't have a service that goes directly to God," Maizie murmured, hanging up.

Mission San Juan Capistrano it was.

Chapter Seven

Nikki doubled back to her house a total of three times before she finally managed to make it out of her development. Once because she'd forgotten her car keys, once because she'd left behind the dessert she was bringing—a rum-flavored Bundt cake that Theresa had insisted on making for her when the woman had heard, via her mother, that she was having dinner at someone's house—and once because she'd driven away without packing the laptop and had only realized it five minutes into her trip.

She knew if she decided not to go back for the laptop, Lucas would insist on coming by to pick it up himself. Judging by the tension in her stomach, this was already feeling more like a date than just a casual get-together.

Having Lucas stop by her house, or even the office without needing to see her as his baby's pediatrician, would feel much too personal.

Would? a small voice inside her head questioned. Newsflash. It already did.

Nikki wasn't up on Freudian theory in general, but she recalled that the pioneering psychiatrist had maintained that there were no such things as accidents. That meant that she was trying to tell herself something by "accidentally" forgetting her keys, and then her dessert, and finally, her laptop.

Maybe she should just stay home. She could call Lucas and use the excuse that something had come up so she had to rush off to the hospital. Sorry about that.

That wasn't going to work.

Lucas already knew she wasn't on call. He'd mentioned the fact that she might be called away when he'd phoned this morning to run the "menu" by her. He wanted to be sure that she didn't have any food allergies or that he hadn't picked the "one thing you hate to eat" to prepare tonight.

When she'd commented that he was far more sensitive and careful than the usual father she came across in her practice, he'd laughed it off, saying, "I've got half a dozen books on baby care and how to raise a healthy kid on my shelves. Reading them has made me a great deal more aware of a lot of things," he'd told her. "Oh, and don't worry if you suddenly have to take off for the hospital. I promise I won't take it personally."

For a second, she'd thought he was making a joke about her not liking his cooking, then realized that Lucas was talking about her being on call.

"I won't be running off," she'd answered. "I'm not on call this weekend." The words were out before she'd realized that she'd just walked all over the perfect excuse to call off dinner.

Because she didn't really want to.

And why should she? How often did she get to enjoy the company of a decent, good-looking man without having to worry that the evening might wind up leading her on to thin ice? That she'd be on her way to a place where decisions were going to have to be made down the line?

There was blissfully no pressure here. Lucas was too devoted to his daughter, too wrapped up around her welfare and his career to leave any room for sexual tension. Tonight would just be about two people enjoying each other's company and the company of his daughter over dinner. No matter how she sliced it, it was a win-win situation.

She had to learn to relax.

There were no ulterior motives to worry about, no holding up her guard in case the man decided to come on strong. He wouldn't. She could literally feel it in her bones.

What could go wrong in a situation like that?

Plenty, it turned out. Just nothing she would have anticipated.

Her first clue came as she parked her car in the

driveway and walked up to the front door. Picking up a noise, Nikki cocked her head to listen. She thought she heard Heather crying.

And then she *definitely* heard something. The sound of a pot or a pan loudly crashing on to a tiled floor jarred her teeth.

Slightly nervous about what she might find, Nikki rang the doorbell. Three times. She waited to the count of ten between each interval, but she might as well have waited to the count of a thousand. The door didn't move and there was no response.

The problem, she thought, was that the doorbell chimes were much too soft to compete with all the other noises that were going on.

Taking out her cell phone, Nikki pressed seven numbers on the keypad.

"Please, Heather, not now," Lucas pleaded as he ran cold water full blast over his stinging hands. He was trying to minimize the burning sensation he felt, maybe even decrease the blisters that he knew were forming.

On the floor near his feet was the nine-by-twelve pan—now half empty—that he'd just taken out of the oven. It hadn't been half empty when he'd put it in, but when smoke had started seeping out of the stove, he'd thrown open the oven door and made a grab for the pan before he had a possible fire on his hands.

Unfortunately, he'd neglected to perform the operation using oven mitts.

The jolting contact with the hot pan caused him to drop it, which in turn sent half the burnt vegetables racing through the kitchen as if they, too, were trying to escape the smoking oven. The smoke alarm was already announcing its displeasure, the pitch high enough to loosen his teeth.

Heather's crying on top of everything else was almost enough to push him over the edge. He knew it was useless, but he tried reasoning with her as if she was older and could understand him.

"I promise I'll get to you in a few minutes. I just need to figure out what other vegetables I can serve." Rushing to the window over the sink, he threw it open, hoping that was enough to get rid of the smell before the doctor got there.

Lucas knew it was futile. Heather's doctor was due at any minute. There just wasn't enough time to clear the air, much less start a new side dish, or whatever the hell they call these things in those cooking shows he sometimes kept on in the background for company while he worked.

Actually, it wasn't even the cooking shows he kept on. He'd switch on any morning show on one of the major channels just to hear the sound of people's voices in conversation. When Heather napped, the house became much too silent. As a rule, he didn't do his best work in silence.

On those occasions that Heather napped while he was working and he wasn't on a conference call, Lucas tended to feel like a hermit.

An inept hermit, he thought in disgust, still running the water over his throbbing fingers.

He didn't know where to start first. Did he clean up the floor, open more windows, start another vegetable—if he even *found* another vegetable to start—or see what was bothering Heather *this* time?

Outnumbered and overwhelmed, Lucas did none of the above. Instead, Lucas glared at the landline as it began to ring, adding to the cacophony.

Now what? He wasn't exactly in the mood to be sociable.

Leaning over, he yanked the receiver from its cradle with one hand. The next second, he was grabbing hold of the edge of the sink with his other hand to keep from slipping on the grease that had spilled on the floor along with the vegetables. His arm felt as if he'd pulled it out of the socket.

"Yes?" he barked into the receiver.

"Lucas?" the female voice on the other end asked uncertainly.

Oh, God, it was her. Heather's doctor. The woman was early.

No, he realized, glancing at the kitchen clock, she was right on time. *He* was late. An hour late by his calculation.

How had that happened? He used to be so organized....

He should have just sent out for pizza, not tried to whip up something of his own, he upbraided himself.

"Hi," he said, trying his best to sound chipper and

not as if he was about to have a major breakdown. "Where are you?"

Mentally, he crossed his fingers, hoping that she was calling to say she hadn't left her house yet. Or, better yet, that she'd had to put in an appearance at the hospital because one of her patients had suddenly been admitted and she estimated that she wouldn't be over for an hour.

An hour would give him enough time to air out the house and perform a minor miracle.

Hopes for a miracle, minor or otherwise, died abruptly when she answered his question. "I'm standing at your front door."

He looked in the direction of the front of the house as if he'd suddenly been given the gift of X-ray vision and could see through the door.

"Why didn't you ring?" Before hurrying over to open the door, he opened the belt that had been holding Heather in her high chair. She'd been sitting there, observing the fiasco he'd unintentionally created, until she'd decided to be part of the noise. Now Heather appeared to be more curious than cranky. The phone tucked against his ear and neck, Lucas lifted Heather up out of the high chair.

"I did," Nikki answered. "Three times." Impatient to come in, she asked, "Lucas, is there any reason why we're conducting a telephone conversation when we're about twenty yards apart?" Why wasn't he letting her in? "Is something wrong?"

Now there was an understatement. Out loud, he was quick to voice a denial. "No, no, nothing's wrong."

He did his best to sound confident and innocent as he hurried to the door now, holding Heather on his hip with one hand, the phone with the other.

"Is that Heather crying in the background?" Nikki asked a beat before the door opened, still speaking into the phone. In response, she heard a garbled noise.

And then the door opened. The first thing she saw was Heather.

About to utter a greeting, Nikki wound up coughing as the smoke from inside the house came out to embrace her, wrapping itself around her like an old friend at a college reunion.

"Oh, my God," Nikki cried in between coughing and trying to catch her breath. Wide-eyed, she looked at him. "Was there a fire?"

"Not exactly," Lucas answered, feeling as if he was the owner of three left hands in a strictly right-handed world.

Not exactly. Nikki's eyes began to smart. "Well, if that's your new air freshener, I'd go back to the store and get my money back if I were you."

Making her way into the house, Nikki found the smoke growing increasingly thicker. She began to open windows on her way to the kitchen. Once there, she saw the haphazardly scattered vegetables on the floor. Quartered potatoes, diced asparagus and string beans, tiny carrots and mushrooms all tossed—*really* tossed—with olive oil and a powdery substance she took to be some kind of cheese, or maybe flour.

She slanted a look in Lucas's direction. "I take it you were planning to be informal."

"Not that informal," he answered. It was obvious that he was really annoyed with himself for being caught like this.

She surveyed the vegetables more closely. They looked fairly well done—that nice, crispy look where the vegetables were not too crunchy, not too soft.

"Well, if it's any consolation to you," she told him, "what you were making looks as if it would have been very tasty."

"It was—until the oil spilled on to the bottom of the oven and started smoking," he told her. "I took the pan out immediately so I could try to clean up the oil before it filled the whole room—"

Nikki looked at the floor and the vegetables. A picture began to emerge. "Let me guess, you forgot to use pot holders and dropped the pan."

Lucas sighed. "That about covers it," he admitted with a nod.

"Why don't you put Heather into her high chair and we'll get started on cleaning up the floor?" she suggested gently.

He looked at the baby. "She's still crying." Although she did sound as if that was abating. "You don't think she's getting sick again, do you?"

Nikki brushed her hand against the baby's forehead. It was cool, and the baby was settling down.

"I think the loud noise scared her more than anything

else," she guessed. With that, she looked around the room, glancing toward the corners. "Where do you keep your mop and your broom?" she asked. Turning around to face him, she saw Lucas wince as he put the baby back into her high chair. He withdrew his hands from his daughter somewhat awkwardly. "Let me see that," she ordered.

"See what?" he asked, dropping his hands to his sides as if to try to divert attention from them.

"Your hands." She looked at him knowingly. "You burned them, didn't you?"

Lucas shrugged his shoulders, deliberately looking away and ignoring her request. He would have slid them into his pockets if doing so wouldn't have hurt like hell. "They're okay."

"No, they're not," she countered. When he looked at her, about to open his mouth in protest, she cut him off with, "Who's the one with a medical degree here?"

"You."

"Exactly." She put her hand out expectantly. "Now let me see them."

She waited, giving no indication that she was about to give up until she saw his hands. With a reluctant sigh, he held them out and turned them over, palms up, for her to examine.

Looking at his hands, it was Nikki's turn to wince as she anticipated the initial pain he had to be experiencing.

"Oh, God, that must smart."

Lucas frowned in self-disgust. He wasn't ordinarily

this inept or this clumsy. Why had he had to pick to-night to start?

"It's probably the only part of me that is," he muttered under his breath.

Nikki laughed softly as she quickly scanned the damage. It wasn't as bad as she'd thought at first glance. Very gently, she lowered his hands to his sides.

"Don't be so hard on yourself, Lucas," she said. And then she nodded toward the door. "I'm going to go out to my car—"

"To make good your escape?" he guessed. He wouldn't blame her if she did.

"No, I have something for burns in the trunk of my car and I'm going to go get it. I like to keep a first aid kit handy at all times." She glanced down at the hand closest to her. "You never know when you might need it. Be right back," she promised.

A couple of minutes later, she was. Opening up a small, see-through box she dipped a cotton ball into its contents and then liberally dabbed a yellowish powder to his fingers.

Bracing himself for more pain, Lucas was surprised when he felt next to none. The powder had taken away a major part of the sting immediately.

"What is that stuff?" he asked, eyeing it curiously as Nikki applied a second layer. "It looks like fairy dust."

She laughed. Fairy dust. She rather liked that. Calling it fairy dust would make it a lot easier to apply to children's skinned hands and knees when it was necessary.

"You've been reading too many fairy tales to Heather. This is just a little compound the doctor I trained under when I was an intern shared with me. There's cornstarch in it and a few other ingredients you can get over the counter at any pharmacy." She regarded the yellowish powder still in the container. "Not impressive-looking, I'll agree, but it really works." She'd used it herself so she could vouch for its effectiveness firsthand. "You should be almost as good as new in a few hours."

Realizing she was still holding one of his hands in hers, Nikki released it, doing her best to appear nonchalant. She didn't want the man thinking she was guilty of holding his hand for no reason.

"The good news is, you really didn't do that much damage to your hands."

Lucas nodded, still feeling like an idiot. He looked his hands over, marveling, "They're not hurting as much as before." He raised his eyes to hers. "I keep saying thank-you."

"You can stop anytime now," she told him with a smile. Nikki closed the little container and then handed it to him. "If it starts to sting again, apply another layer. Better safe than sorry," she added when he looked at her quizzically.

"Don't you need it?" he asked.

"I have more," she told him. "Don't worry, it's not like it's made out of a magic root that only grows once every fifty years."

Snapping the first aid kit shut, Nikki slid off the stool.

The Reader Service—Here's how it works: Accepting your 2 free books and 2 free gifts (gifts valued at approximately $10.00) places you under no obligation to buy anything. You may keep the books and gifts and return the shipping statement marked "cancel". If you do not cancel, about a month later we'll send you 6 additional books and bill you just $4.24 each in the U.S. or $4.99 each in Canada. That is a savings of 15% off the cover price. It's quite a bargain! Shipping and handling is just 50¢ per book in the U.S. and 75¢ per book in Canada.* You may cancel at any time, but if you choose to continue, every month we'll send you 6 more books, which you may either purchase at the discount price or return to us and cancel your subscription.
*Terms and prices subject to change without notice. Prices do not include applicable taxes. Sales tax applicable in N.Y. Canadian residents will be charged applicable provincial taxes and GST. Offer not valid in Quebec. Credit or debit balances in a customer's account(s) may be offset by any other outstanding balance owed by or to the customer. Please allow 4 to 6 weeks for delivery. Offer available while quantities last. All orders subject to approval.

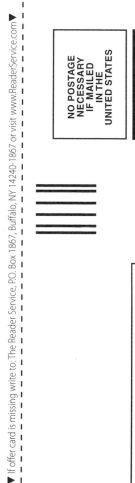

▶ If offer card is missing write to: The Reader Service, P.O. Box 1867, Buffalo, NY 14240-1867 or visit www.ReaderService.com ▶

NO POSTAGE
NECESSARY
IF MAILED
IN THE
UNITED STATES

BUSINESS REPLY MAIL
FIRST-CLASS MAIL   PERMIT NO. 717   BUFFALO, NY

POSTAGE WILL BE PAID BY ADDRESSEE

THE READER SERVICE
PO BOX 1867
BUFFALO NY 14240-9952

Send For
2 FREE BOOKS
Today!

I accept your offer!

Please send me two free *Silhouette Special Edition*® novels and two mystery gifts (gifts worth about $10). I understand that these books are completely free—even the shipping and handling will be paid—and I am under no obligation to purchase anything, ever, as explained on the back of this card.

About how many NEW paperback fiction books have you purchased in the past 3 months?

❏ 0-2	❏ 3-6	❏ 7 or more
E4LM	E4LX	E4MA

235/335 SDL

Please Print

FIRST NAME

LAST NAME

ADDRESS

APT.#	CITY

STATE/PROV.	ZIP/POSTAL CODE

Visit us online at
www.ReaderService.com

Offer limited to one per household and not valid to current subscribers of Silhouette Special Edition® books.

Your Privacy—Silhouette Books is committed to protecting your privacy. Our Privacy Policy is available online at www.eHarlequin.com or upon request from the Reader Service. From time to time we make our list of customers available to reputable third parties who may have a product or service of interest to you. If you would prefer for us not to share your name and address, please check here ❏ **Help us get it right**—We strive for accurate, respectful and relevant communications. To clarify or modify your communication preferences, visit us at www.ReaderService.com/consumerschoice.

© 2009 HARLEQUIN ENTERPRISES LIMITED. ® and ™ are trademarks owned and used by the trademark owner and/or its licensee. Printed in the U.S.A.

▲ Detach card and mail today. No stamp needed. ▲

S-SE-03/10

Heather, fascinated by what was going on, had completely stopped fussing and watched everything now with her huge blue eyes.

Lucas was very aware of the fact that, although his hands might not be hurting as much as they first had, the kitchen still looked as if it had been hit by a mini hurricane.

"Why don't you entertain Heather and I'll clean up?" he suggested to Nikki.

But Nikki shook her head. "That would necessitate you using your hands and it would be better for you if you just let the 'fairy dust' sink in. Why don't we switch assignments? That way, you can entertain your daughter and I'll clean up."

That didn't seem fair at all. He hadn't invited her over just to put her to work. He was supposed to be repaying her for what she'd done for Heather.

"Won't I need my hands to entertain Heather?" he questioned.

"Make faces," she instructed, deliberately using a deadpan, serious voice. "That way, you don't have to touch her."

Lucas laughed. "Are you *ever* at a loss for an answer?"

Lots of times, Nikki thought. She was at a loss as to why she always seemed to have a tendency to gravitate to proverbial bad-boy types, even though she knew that things would only go badly for her at the end.

But out loud, she merely grinned at his question and told him, "I'll let you know."

"That's what I thought." Angling his daughter's high chair closer to him, he slid on to a stool, watching the doctor.

As was Heather, he noted.

Meanwhile, her pediatrician had located a broom and had begun cornering the runaway vegetables, curtailing their freedom.

Lucas shook his head. "I really feel guilty about you having to do this."

"You could feel guilty," she told him, scanning the room for a dustpan, "only if you planned this."

Sensing what she was looking for, he pointed under the sink, to the left. When she opened the door, she found the dustpan *and* the garbage. Not exactly a trifecta but it would do.

"If you *didn't* plan this stint of labor, then there's no reason to feel that way. Accidents, despite what Freud thought to the contrary—" she felt compelled to add "—can and do happen. There's no real harm done," Nikki assured him, nodding at the floor.

Very quickly, she rounded up the vegetables, sending them into an orderly pile.

The next minute, as if to prove her theory about the randomness of accidents, Nikki felt her feet suddenly start to go out from under her as if she was ice-skating on the tile.

Chapter Eight

Nikki's sudden, surprised gasp slipped out at the same time and mingled with Lucas's sharp intake of breath as he made a grab for her. The quick, firm contact as he wrapped his fingers around her arms had generated a fresh volley of stinging pain through them.

It all happened so fast.

Grabbing her arms to keep Nikki from falling down and hurting herself, Lucas instinctively pulled her to him. And then, time, which had been zooming by, suddenly seemed to slip into a heated, almost trance-like slow-motion pace. One second, he was making a grab for the woman, the next, he'd pulled her up to him until her body was completely against his. There was not so much as room for a breath between them.

They were all but sealed together.

His fingers weren't stinging anymore, at least not that he could notice. But an ache of a different kind definitely existed, materializing out of nothing and growing prodigiously.

Her breath was against his face. It smelled sweet. Enticing. Stirring up other, long-dormant sensations within him.

Was it longing?

Lucas wasn't sure.

Wasn't sure of anything right now, except that his knees had grown strangely wobbly.

He could have sworn that not only was there no space for anyone or anything else in his life beyond his daughter, but he would have made a fairly high bet, wagering the sum of his bank account and the roof over his head— he was that certain—that he was never going to feel anything remotely approaching a sexual reaction to another woman ever again.

Carole had been his world. They'd grown up together. On both sides of the marriage. They'd played as children, they'd played in a different way as young adults. He had firmly believed that Carole was the only woman for him. From a very young age, he'd been certain of that.

It hadn't even occurred to him to look around, to "sample" being with other women. He didn't want to "sample," he just knew. He was a one-woman man and Carole had been that woman.

And yet, right here, right now, Lucas was keenly aware that he was wondering what it would feel like to kiss his daughter's doctor.

Was he going crazy?

She stood very, very still, hardly drawing a breath. An electricity crackled between them, Nikki could swear to it. Like an unexpected summer storm, it had come out of nowhere, bursting on top of her before she even realized that there was a cloud in the sky, much less that it was directly overhead.

What did she do? Did she give in to the almost overwhelming attraction and kiss him? Or did she force herself to take a step back, hoping that distance would somehow help to cool what was clearly her critically overheated jets?

If she gave in, it wouldn't exactly be orthodox, but then again, it wasn't as if Lucas Wingate was her patient. It was his daughter she'd treated and this was really a social visit, not a professional one. She was here as a "friend," not a doctor.

A friend staring into an incredibly gray area.

So what are you going to do? You can't just stand here forever like some statue. Do something.

And then, to Nikki's overwhelming relief and surprise, the ultimate decision was taken away from her. Lucas had freed her of the responsibility. Slipping his hands into her hair and framing her face with a movement as soft and as gentle as a whisper, Lucas touched his lips to hers.

At first, it was just the barest of contacts, but then the contact grew, blossomed, flowered into something that wasn't just fleeting, but something that left an imprint on her soul. An imprint that went far deeper than his lips initially had.

The kiss stole both her breath and her concept of time away, igniting a flame within the campsite of her feelings that she could have sworn had long since just died out. Her blood surged and a fragment of some catchy melody circled around in her brain.

For the first time in two years—maybe longer—she felt alive. Alive, and really, really confused.

She shouldn't be doing this.

But she liked it.

She *more* than liked it.

Her heart pounded, sending messages to every inch of her body by the time the kiss ended and Lucas finally took a step back, creating a space between them. Nikki realized that she couldn't go anywhere. Her back was pinned by the stool that was built against the counter.

At least she couldn't fall down, she thought. Very carefully, Nikki took a deep breath, trying to steady her erratic pulse.

"If that was supposed to get my mind off dinner," she began slowly, doing her best not to sound breathless, "it succeeded."

His laugh in response had just the tiniest hint of awkwardness to it. In all honesty, he had no idea what the kiss was supposed to accomplish. He'd kind of fallen headlong into it himself. The only thing he really did know was that it succeeded in confusing the hell out of him.

He'd acted, he realized, not only out of character for him, but more to the point, out of his mind. He was unendingly grateful that she hadn't gotten angry or demanded to know what the hell he thought he was doing. He had absolutely no experience in going with his gut.

She might still become angry, he thought.

Lucas grasped at the first topic that occurred to him in hopes of diverting her attention from what had just happened. "Why don't we order pizza so that the evening's not a total loss?"

Her eyes met his for a long, pregnant moment. "Oh, the evening's not a loss," she assured him quietly, thinking to herself that she'd just uttered one of the biggest understatements of her life. "But I have to admit that pizza does sound pretty good."

Especially since, as it turned out, there wasn't all that much to salvage on the dinner front. There was nothing inside the stove or the microwave. She had a feeling that Lucas had neglected to remember to make a main course. Tactfully, she refrained from asking about it.

Lucas took the number to the closest pizzeria down from the refrigerator where a magnet had held it securely in place.

"What's your favorite kind of pizza?" he asked as he reached for the telephone.

"Flat."

He laughed. The woman couldn't be this easy, could she? "Can I have a little more to go on?"

Nikki shrugged. "Add anything you want," she told him. "If it's pizza, I'll eat it." But that, she realized, wasn't exactly true. "Except maybe if they want to put on pineapples."

Well, at least it was something. "Not a fan of pineapples?" he asked, amused.

"I like pineapples just fine—just not on pizza." She worked as she talked, discovering that kissing Lucas had given her an incredible surge of energy she needed to work out of her system.

She carefully swept up the last of the vegetables then ran a mop over the area to prevent another mishap— although a repeat performance of sliding into his arms was not without its charm.

"God made pizza to taste chewy and tangy with all that cheese and sauce on it. And sausage," she added belatedly. "It seems like a sacrilege to smother all that taste with pineapple chunks."

Lucas attempted to hide his amusement. "And there's no negotiating this?"

It suddenly occurred to her, as she put the mop and broom away and dusted off her hands, that Heather's father might be a fan of Hawaiian pizza. She didn't want to dictate what they were having for dinner. She just wouldn't eat that much of it.

"I'm sorry," she apologized. "I didn't mean to sound

so rigid. This is your house. You should be able to get whatever you want."

He was tempted to comment on that, but he didn't. Instead, he fell back on basic etiquette. "But you're the guest."

"The unintentionally fussy guest," she pointed out. "Please, don't let me sway you. Get anything you like."

The thought occurred to him that he already had. A wave of warmth enveloped him. Lucas kept the thought to himself.

Turning from the sink where she'd just washed her hands, Nikki saw the somewhat reddish hue that was working across his face.

Men blushed?

She didn't think so. It was warm in here. She'd felt a wave a moment ago herself. That would explain why he'd flushed.

Their eyes met and Nikki realized that he knew what she was thinking. A last minute save had her making a joke out of it.

"Obviously the idea of a naked pizza—except for the stringy cheese—turns you on."

Lucas found himself growing at ease again. "Is that what you want?"

"Naked pizza or to turn you on?"

Hearing her own voice utter the words nearly made her clap her hands over her mouth. She had no idea what had prompted her to say that. She was not the type to push anything on a private level in any manner, shape or form. And she wasn't the type to just blurt things out or be blunt.

Right now, she thought, the less she said, the better the situation was for both of them.

With that one snappy-sexy line she'd inadvertently uttered, she'd just killed any chance of keeping what had transpired between them quiet, hoping to have it die a natural death.

Clearing her throat, Nikki focused on food. Of the two, it was definitely the safer topic. "Pizza, I was thinking of the pizza, of course."

"Of course," he echoed.

Lucas had no idea why he felt so much like smiling, even as he found himself wrestling to stuff newly escaped feelings back into the box they'd just leaped out of. He had strong suspicions that he wasn't going to be having much luck with that effort tonight. Consequently, he went to Plan B: ignoring those feelings. As thoroughly as he could manage.

Picking up the receiver, he hit the numbers on the keypad that would connect him to the closest pizzeria.

Nikki took the small amount of vegetables that had survived the fall and remained in the pan, transferring them into a bowl. She placed the pan into the sink and filled it with sudsy water. As she cleaned, she heard Lucas ordering two large pizzas, both with extra mozzarella cheese.

Looking for a towel to dry her hands, she came up empty. She used a paper towel instead.

"Two?" she questioned, crossing to the wastebasket and throwing the paper towel away. "Just how hungry are you?"

Until just a few minutes ago, he hadn't realized how hungry he was.

But he was going to have to put that into perspective, he warned himself. If you hadn't had water in seven months, the first taste of water might make you act irrationally. Any attractive woman's kiss would have sent his head spinning. It had nothing to do with Heather's doctor.

Focus, Wingate.

"Cold pizza the next morning has always been one of my favorite breakfasts," he told her.

She smiled at that. "Contains all the basic food groups," she agreed, straight-faced. "So, then you were stocking up."

He opened a jar of strained bananas and took out a spoon to feed Heather. "Something like that." He began to sit down, but Nikki took both the spoon and the jar from him and sat down in his chair. "They promised to get here in twenty minutes or less."

"That's fast," she commented. Making a silly face to entertain Heather, she slipped the first semifull spoon between the rosebud lips.

"Not really. The pizzeria is on the other side of this development. They take a short cut to get here." Watching her feed his daughter, he marveled at her precision. How did she manage to get so much into Heather's mouth instead of on her face and bib? There had to be a trick to it and he for one was not above taking lessons. Whenever he fed his daughter, he was lucky if half the jar made it into her mouth. It was usually less than that.

Another spoonful went in. "You've ordered from them before."

"A number of times." He continued watching. There was hardly *any* of the strained banana getting on the bib. He doubted that he could ever approach being that good. "What gave me away?"

She glanced at him over her shoulder as she fed Heather. "The grin of anticipation."

Lucas wasn't aware that he was grinning, but if he was, it wasn't because of the pizza that was about to arrive. But that was something else he decided was better if he kept to himself.

He couldn't keep shoving things under the rug. Eventually, there'd be a bump under it big enough to trip him and send him sprawling. Best to nip it in the bud before it got to those proportions.

Taking a breath, Lucas cleared his throat. "Listen, about before—"

Nikki instantly became alert. She didn't want Lucas to feel as if he was on the spot and that she wanted him to explain. Conversely, she didn't want to be on the spot, either. She hadn't been the one to initiate the kiss, but she hadn't pulled away either, and circumstances were a little murky, but she might have been the one to perpetuate the kiss.

"No need to say anything," she told Lucas cheerfully as she fed an animated Heather the last of her strained banana. "Sometimes, things just happen without any rhyme or reason."

That kind of explanation applied to shifts in the weather, not to him. If anything, he was too predictable. It had been Carole's only complaint about him and yet, at the same time, it was one of his qualities, she'd told him, that she liked. It comforted her to know him inside and out, to know that he wasn't unpredictable and that she could depend on him because she knew that whatever he did, it would be true to form. True to her.

"Things might," he allowed, "but I don't."

Nikki got up, leaving cleanup to him while she washed out the baby's spoon. "Sure you do," she insisted. "You just did." Heather made a squealing noise. "You can't still be hungry," Nikki protested, then saw what it was that the baby was trying to "tell" them. Heather was blowing bubbles, creating them out of the excess saliva that was in her mouth. Nikki knew what that was all about.

She turned toward Lucas. "I'll leave you some more of that numbing solution for her gums," Nikki promised. "Otherwise, you're going to have another sleepless night, maybe even tonight."

"You see another one breaking through?" he asked, coming up behind her to look into Heather's mouth in order to see for himself.

"No, it's not breaking through yet."

"Then how—?"

"Bubbles," she pointed out. "Heather's drooling again. Remember what that means? Babies drool when they're teething."

All of this was still pretty much a mystery to him, he thought, wondering if he was *ever* going to get the hang of it completely. "Right," he agreed, then confessed, "I forgot."

"Don't worry," she assured him easily. "You have a lot on your mind. This'll all be old hat to you eventually."

"By the time it is, she'll have grown past teething and cutting teeth," he lamented.

"And on to another phase," Nikki promised. "At this age, it's all about phases. They go from one to another like social butterflies table hopping at a charity function. It'll get to the point that you think it'll never end." She flashed a grin at the uncertain, somewhat hopeless look that crossed Lucas's face. "That's how they separate the strong dads from the ones who can't make it." Without thinking, she gave his shoulder a quick pat. "My money's on you."

Too bad he didn't share her confidence. He already felt like a man who was very close to drowning. "I never realized that parenting could be so hard."

That didn't surprise her. "That's because you're the male parent."

He looked at her, confused. "And that makes a difference?"

"Damn straight it does," she said with feeling. Even in this day and age, she'd listened to her share of mothers complaining about their husbands. "Male parents get to pass the buck at this stage, letting their female counterparts handle everything except for the essentially sweet things, like tucking the babies into bed and watching them sleep."

"I don't have anyone to pass the buck to," he pointed out.

He'd tried to gloss over the sorrow, but she'd heard it nonetheless. "I know and I'm sorry about that. But—" Nikki brightened "—on the plus side, you get to experience everything and be there for all the special times you might have otherwise missed."

Heather picked that moment to have her face take on a shade of beet-red. Hands clenched, she made a straining, grunting noise. The air around her suddenly turned very pungent.

"Like that?" Lucas asked, looking at Nikki pointedly.

"Like that," Nikki conceded. The little girl definitely needed changing. Quickly. "Because I'm in a generous mood, I'll spot you one," Nikki offered. She glanced toward the stairs. The nursery was upstairs. "You keep her diapers in her room?" It was a rhetorical question.

"After the last time you were here, you should know better than I do," Lucas told her. After all, the woman had been the one who had organized everything in what had seemed like lightning speed. Luckily, he hadn't allowed things to get away from him too much yet.

"Just checking," Nikki replied, then turned to Heather. She began to undo the straps that were holding the little girl in her high chair. "C'mon, princess. Let's get you smelling pretty again." Lifting the small tray that was in front of Heather, Nikki angled the little girl out of the high chair and scooped her up into her arms. Just then, the doorbell pealed. "You weren't kidding about them taking a shortcut," she commented, glancing at her watch. "It hasn't even been fifteen minutes since you placed the order." Now that she thought of it, she *was* pretty hungry. "I can feel my mouth watering already," she told him as she walked out of the room with Heather tucked against her shoulder.

Lucas watched her leave for a moment.

So can I, Lucas silently said to the departed physician's back.

And then he hurried over to the door, doing his best to block out any other thoughts. It was obvious that his common sense had taken the night off.

Chapter Nine

Thinking was highly overrated, Nikki decided later that night. Spending too much time at it just led to false starts and massive confusion.

The latter place was where she was right now.

The few times that she'd actually been attracted to someone beyond a fleeting infatuation, she'd just gone with the feeling instead of holding it under the microscope and examining it from every conceivable side. She hadn't wondered if she was reading things into the actions of the person she was drawn to. She didn't waste time speculating if the hoofbeats she heard belonged to a horse or a zebra—she'd just gone with horse every time.

And ultimately wound up having her heart badly trampled.

This time around, she was afraid to make a move, afraid to enjoy what was happening because, burnt more than once and convinced that all her luck with men was bad, she was anxious that she might be misreading signs again. Anxious that she might be deluding herself as to where things could eventually go.

At the end of the evening, after she and Lucas had done justice to the pizza, put Heather to bed and talked for what seemed like hours, Lucas had walked her to her car, waited for her to unlock the driver's side door and then held it open for her.

What he didn't do was kiss her.

It was then that she realized that she'd really wanted him to, despite the fact that if he did, it would have *really* complicated things. As it stood right now, the unexpected kiss in the kitchen was just a function of time and place, not necessarily opportunity or even desire.

As she made peace with her disappointment, she knew that in addition to that disappointment she was also somewhat relieved that he hadn't kissed her again because if he had, it would have seriously jarred their footing. Right now, they were still pediatrician and patient's father, not two people on the possible brink of something a great deal more complicated.

But what if…

Nikki sighed as she stared at the shadows growing larger on her bedroom ceiling. The full moon seemed determined to push its way into her room. Just as determined as her thoughts were to go on a wild goose chase.

"Damn it, Nik, just enjoy the moment and stop thinking about what it might mean in the bigger scheme of things," she chided out loud.

If men could enjoy spending time with a woman, no strings attached, no attachments implied, why couldn't she just enjoy spending time with Lucas? He appeared to be a warm, caring father—clearly out of his element and in over his head, but still a warm, caring father. And he was interesting, intelligent and funny. She liked talking to him, liked his company. *And* she wasn't at a place where she needed things to become serious, no matter what her mother said to the contrary. She had time. Lots of time.

What's more, she didn't need a man to complete her. She liked herself just the way she was.

That settled—she hoped—Nikki turned on her side. If she didn't get some sleep soon, she was going to be a zombie tomorrow and then all those chores that she'd planned to catch up on were just going to continue piling up and becoming less and less manageable.

Forty-five minutes later, after tossing and turning enough to scramble her sheets beneath her, Nikki finally fell asleep.

Nikki wound up sleeping in, although she hadn't intended to when she'd originally made her plans for the day. Her body was so overjoyed at being able to remain horizontal for longer than four hours at a clip, she decided to stay that way just a little longer.

The next thing she knew, three more hours had gone by.

Startled when the numbers on the nightstand clock registered, Nikki bolted upright. She was about to spring out of bed when she realized, belatedly, that it was Sunday, not Monday.

She wasn't due anywhere for any reason, although she supposed that she should give her mother a call— or at least call Theresa to thank her for the cake the woman had made for her to bring to Lucas's house. The rum-flavored bundt cake wasn't exactly the first thing someone thought of as going with pizza, but it still tasted out of this world. It made her really wish that she was as creative in the kitchen as Theresa was, but her abilities began and ended with setting the microwave timer.

She glanced at the phone, debating calling her mother's friend.

Maybe later, when her brain didn't feel so foggy and she was up to fielding the inevitable questions that would come her way.

Nikki knew that if she called Theresa, Theresa would call her mother the moment she hung up. That was how the Mother Grapevine worked. Theresa, Cecilia and her mother were lifelong friends who watched out for each other and, more to the point, watched out for each other's daughters. Her mother was the fiercest one at this game, but Theresa and Cecilia were no slouches, either.

Right now, she didn't feel up to taking questions—even politely worded questions—because she was no less confused this morning as she had been last night.

Although, in the light of day, Nikki realized that from a professional point of view, the right thing had happened. They'd said good-night and gone their separate ways. If, in time, they became good friends, that was fine. A lot of her patients' parents thought of her as a friend, someone to turn to and lean on during mystifying phases of their children's lives.

She'd encouraged that actually, because she liked the country-doctor aspect of medicine that had all but disappeared from existence in the face of modern technology. None of her patients' fathers were potentially something more than just parents. That was going to have to be true of Lucas as well. The line that had been temporarily breeched last night was back in place by the end of the evening.

God, she thought as she went off to the shower, was in His heaven and all was right with the world.

Except for her coffeemaker, Nikki thought darkly some thirty minutes later as she stared at the defunct machine. After several attempts to turn it off and on, then unplugging and plugging it back in, the coffeemaker still refused to brew or to even show any sort of signs of life.

Well, she thought in exasperation, she'd showered and was dressed in jeans and a T-shirt. She supposed that there was nothing wrong with getting into her car and driving to a coffee shop—or even stopping at a fast-food place. There was one close by that had revamped its breakfast menu and claimed to now sell coffee that didn't taste as if someone had boiled black crayons to achieve the right color.

Nikki frowned at the coffeemaker, giving it a sound whack on the side in one last attempt to jar it back into productive service. The only thing that happened was that the water she'd poured in sloshed from side to side. A little spilled out on to the counter. But the major portion of the water remained in the urn, refusing to even entertain a nodding acquaintance with the coffee granules she'd put into the filter.

Nikki glared at the inert coffeemaker. What *was* it with machines and her? Vacuum cleaners seemed to die a premature death whenever she bought one and used it. Computers developed viruses—

Computers.

Oh, God, she'd left her laptop at Lucas's house last night, she suddenly remembered. Between the fiasco with the vegetables, feeding Heather for Lucas and sharing the pizza, they hadn't even gotten around to talking about the computer's problems. She'd brought it into the house with her and then promptly forgot about it.

Especially after that unexpected, temperature-raising kiss.

Lucas was going to think she was an idiot. Either that, or devious, leaving the laptop so she had an excuse to see him again. Right now, she preferred that he thought of her as an idiot. She definitely didn't want the man to lump her in with women who went out of their way to play those insipid male-female games.

What did it matter what he thought, she silently demanded the next minute. *She* knew she wasn't playing games and she wasn't in the market for anything— except for success when it came to her practice.

Nikki chewed on her bottom lip. So what did she do? Did she call Lucas and mention the laptop? Or did she let it slide until at least tomorrow? It wasn't as if she and her laptop were inseparable. She wasn't one of those people who felt a compelling need to check her e-mail every fifteen minutes. If she should suddenly be overcome with an overwhelming need to read her e-mail, she could always go to the Internet café to catch up. The café was only a couple of miles from here. She was fairly certain that it was open on Sundays.

Besides, she reminded herself, the laptop really wasn't working all that well. That had been the whole reason behind her bringing it to Lucas in the first place.

And the reason behind leaving it? a small voice taunted.

There'd been no reason for that, but there *was* a reason for getting it back, she suddenly remembered. She'd promised to download a paper that one of her friends from medical school had written and asked her to review.

Okay, new problem. Did she call Lucas about the laptop, or call Wendy to tell her she was too busy to read anything this weekend?

Coffee—she needed coffee, Nikki thought, looking at the dormant coffeemaker as her brain bounced back and forth from one thought to another. Coffee shop first, Nikki silently declared, grabbing her keys and her wallet. She wouldn't be needing anything else—

Except to answer the door, Nikki thought in exasperation. The doorbell rang just as she reached for the doorknob.

Please don't let it be my mother.

She felt too scattered right now to be up to any kind of verbal sparring and her mother had the uncanny ability to hone in on that kind of thing. The woman could see right through her and get to the heart of whatever it was that was going on.

It wasn't her mother but the one person responsible for her feeling so up in the air in the first place.

"Forget something?" Lucas asked her in amusement.

Upon seeing her, Heather began to wave her feet in gleeful recognition. Sitting on her father's hip, the little girl leaned as far over as she could to reach for Nikki.

"Hi, little one." Brushing a kiss against the top of the baby's head, Nikki took the baby into her arms. "Name, rank and serial number?" she asked with a hopeful note in her voice, looking at Lucas.

Taken aback, he stared at her as if she'd suddenly lapsed into some elaborate form of unintelligible gibberish.

"What?"

Nikki shook her head, dismissing her admittedly feeble attempt at humor. "Nothing. Just being flippant."

She glanced accusingly over her shoulder toward the kitchen. "I get that way without coffee in the morning."

"Funny you should mention that," he said with a grin. "I've got some in the car."

She was still annoyed with the sudden demise of the coffeemaker and was focused on the machine. "You've got a coffee urn in your car?"

Why would she think that? "No, just a couple of large containers. I stopped at a drive-through," he explained.

Relief swept over her. "Oh, God bless you. Could you bring it in?" she all but pleaded.

"You really like coffee that much?" he asked.

She laughed somewhat self-consciously. "You have no idea."

"No problem. I'll go get it now." With Nikki holding his daughter, his hands were free to bring in what he'd brought over. "I'll bring in your laptop, too. That's what I was referring to just now when I asked you if you'd forgotten something."

So completely it was as if her mind had been erased, Nikki thought. But that was his fault. His and that kiss of his.

Not that she was about to even remotely hint to him that that was the reason.

Instead, she pulled her lips into a generic smile and nodded. "I guess I did. Sorry about that."

"No reason to be sorry," he told her. "I kind of snared your attention with my tossed vegetables trick. Anyway, it's all fixed."

She wasn't following. "What's all fixed?"

"The laptop. You really do have trouble concentrating until you have your coffee, don't you?" The corners of his mouth curved in amusement. "I'll bring in both," he said, walking out again.

She followed him out, unconsciously rocking Heather ever so slightly. "How could you have fixed it?" she asked. "I didn't even show you what the problem was."

"It wasn't exactly a baffling mystery," he told her as he returned. He carried the laptop with one hand and balanced the cardboard tray with two coffee containers with the other. "What happened was that you downloaded some mail that had a hidden Trojan in it. Once you did that, the Trojan let loose a virus that affected the laptop's performance. Lucky for you, whoever did that was an amateur. Someone better at it could have corrupted the whole hard drive and then I would have had to install a new one. All the data you had on there could have been lost."

"But—"

He second-guessed her question. "It wasn't."

That wasn't what she was about to say. "I wouldn't have opened up mail with a virus attached to it," she protested.

He grinned at her innocence. He knew she wasn't a naive woman. She'd struck him as being very intelligent. But there was no such thing as a renaissance person these days and computers were obviously her weak point.

"It's not as if it was flagged. You wouldn't have known it was there," he pointed out gently.

"Oh."

"That's how most viruses are spread. Not as dramatically as it was in that last *Die Hard* movie, but it can do just as much damage," he assured her. "There're viruses out there that can do irreparable damage, affect countless systems and bring them down in seconds. The one your laptop 'caught' is small-time. Think of it as being a gremlin instead of a dragon. This virus's purpose is just to annoy the recipient. Hackers like to play those kinds of games."

She thought of the number of times the whole thing froze on her and she'd had to shut it down only not to get it to reboot.

"Well, whoever did it certainly achieved his goal."

Setting both the laptop and the tray with the coffee containers down on the counter, he took back his daughter. Nikki immediately picked up the coffee container, wrapping both her hands around it. She tipped it back and took a long, sensuous sip. As she swallowed, the hot liquid wound its way down through her system.

Heaven.

She could feel herself becoming human and rational again. A sigh of contentment escaped her lips. She took another long sip, then, putting the container down for a moment, she took a closer look at the laptop. Working with one hand, Lucas had opened it and turned it on.

The screen came on. Blue lights danced around as the machine went through its paces.

The first thing she noticed was that the annoying, intimidating grinding noise was gone.

Respect filtered through the wonder. "And you fixed it?"

The look on her face amused him. He grinned. "I fixed it."

She had no idea where to begin. The computer technician she'd contacted had told her he'd have to take possession of her computer for a week. "So quick?"

It was no big deal as far as Lucas was concerned. "Like I said, it wasn't a very sophisticated virus."

That all depended on your point of view, Nikki thought.

"It was to me," she told him. "I was this close—" she measured out a tiny space with her thumb and forefinger "—to tossing the laptop across the room and stomping on it."

Lucas tried to wrap his head around that image and couldn't. "You just don't strike me as being hot tempered."

"I'm not," she said with conviction. "Usually," Nikki felt compelled to add. When he raised his eyebrow quizzically, she made a full confession. "There's just something about computers and machines in general that bring out the worst in me. I suppose it's only fair, since I seem to bring out the worst in them."

He'd been tinkering with mechanical things and fixing whatever needed fixing since he was a kid. Being inept around electronic gadgetry was inconceivable to him. "Come again?"

"My coffee machine refused to work this morning," she enumerated. "And vacuum cleaners have a habit of dying on me after what, for the average person, is a very short interval. Irons short-circuit and wind up burning things. The life span of an iron around me is just under eight months."

"You iron?"

"Just barely."

"Must be your magnetic personality," he teased. And then he laughed, shaking his head. "I guess it's a lucky thing that you're not a mechanic or a pilot."

Nikki didn't even want to think about that. She'd be labeled a disaster, looking for somewhere to happen. "I guess so." Changing the topic slightly, she asked, "What do I owe you?" When he looked at her blankly, she added, "For fixing the laptop?"

Lucas was surprised that she even thought to ask that. "Nothing. You don't owe me anything."

That didn't seem fair. She would have had to pay the technician who canceled on her. "But—"

"Call it a trade-off," he told her. When he'd reminded her about billing him, she'd said there wouldn't be a bill coming since her office manager wasn't able to place a monetary value on something that they were not in the habit of doing. House calls had gone the way of the dinosaur. "Although," he added, "I clearly got the better end of the deal."

She didn't like being the last recipient, didn't like feeling in debt even if he never made any reference to it again. *She* would know. And knowing made her feel uncomfortable.

"All right, since we're doing turnaround and fair play

and all that, how about I invite you over for dinner?" She looked at the baby. "Both of you."

He didn't have to think about it. "I'd like that."

"Good. How does next Saturday sound? I can get someone to take my place on standby."

His smile widened appreciatively. "Sounds like a plan to me."

Too bad, she thought, that it didn't sound like the same to her. She'd gotten swept away with the idea of payback before she remembered one very crucial thing. She couldn't cook well enough to keep a family of undernourished squirrels alive.

No problem, she tried to reassure herself. She had all of one week to learn how. All she had to do was put her mind to it.

And hope that was enough.

Chapter Ten

"You can't tell Mother."

Silence on the other end of the line met Nikki's request.

The phone call to Theresa was admittedly a last resort kind of thing, but right now, since she'd gone out on a limb with this invitation she'd tendered to Lucas, it was her only recourse. She couldn't go back on the invitation since it was her idea and she couldn't cook. The odds of her learning how by Saturday were rather small. That left having someone "ghost" cook for her. The logical choice was a woman who made her living that way.

She had a great deal of affection for Theresa and thought of her as a quieter version of her mother. But still, the woman had more allegiance to her mother than to her. Placing the call the moment her office closed for lunch, Nikki knew she was asking a lot. She was counting on Theresa's kind heart.

"Theresa, you have to promise me you won't tell Mother. I'll pay you anything you want to make the dinner, just don't say a word to my mother. Please," she pleaded.

She heard Theresa sigh on the other end. "But sweetheart, your mother's my best friend."

"I know, but your best friend will grill me to an inch of my life if you breathe a word of this to her." Nikki sank down in her chair, too tense to sit back. "You know how she is. Besides," she interjected, "it's not what you think."

"It's not?" Theresa made no attempt to hide the blatant curiosity in her voice.

"No," Nikki answered firmly. Maybe this was a mistake, turning to Theresa. Maybe she should have just resorted to takeout from a local restaurant. But Theresa's cooking was fabulous and she did want Lucas to have a good meal. "The parent of one of my patients called me in a panic a couple of weeks ago because his daughter was running a fever. You know, crying, all that incredibly scary, first-time-around stuff. I talked him through it." Okay, so she was omitting a few details, like driving over in the middle of the night, but Theresa didn't need to know that part. "He was so grateful that he invited me over for dinner."

"And now you want to reciprocate?" Theresa guessed knowingly.

"Something like that." Nikki held her breath, waiting to see if there were going to be more probing questions. It went without saying that there would have been if her mother was on the other end instead of Theresa. This whole conversation would have been chock-full of questions.

"And you're afraid of poisoning him."

Oh, good, Theresa understood, Nikki thought, releasing the breath she was holding. "Exactly."

There was a short laugh on the other end. "And what's he going to do to reciprocate this meal? Take out your tonsils with a Swiss Army knife?"

"He won't have to reciprocate. We'll be even, Theresa," Nikki insisted. That was part of the point. "So," she continued, wanting to wrap it up while she still had time to get something to eat, "are you going to do it?"

"Of course I'll cook a dinner for you, Nikki. That's what I do."

She realized she wasn't being clear. Dealing with details that had to do with her mother always seemed to muddle her otherwise crystal-clear thought process. Why was that? "No, I meant, are you going to do it and *not* tell Mother?"

She heard Theresa pause again, as if the older woman was weighing her options. "If you don't want me to tell your mother that I'm catering a small, intimate dinner—"

"Not so intimate," Nikki cut in. If Theresa thought of it in romantic terms, all bets were off. Her mother would know in a heartbeat, even if she didn't admit to anything directly. Her mother could smell dinner for two a mile away. She was uncanny that way.

Theresa went on talking as if nothing had been said. "For you and your patient's father, I won't be the one to tell her."

Had the woman she'd known since she was a little girl been in the room with her, Nikki would have thrown her arms around Theresa and hugged her. Hard. Instead, trying to maintain a composed facade, she said as calmly as she could, "Thank you, Theresa. I knew you'd understand."

"All right. What do you want to serve and how soon do you want to serve it?"

"Nothing fancy. I leave it all up to your fabulous discretion. As for how soon, I'll need it this Saturday." Mentally, she crossed her fingers. "Will that be a problem?"

"No problem at all," Theresa assured her. "Dinner for two I can do standing on my head."

"I'd prefer if you were standing on your feet," Nikki said dryly. "Bless you, Theresa. You're the best. I've got to go now." And she really did. The light on her landline was on. Someone was calling in between hours. "And please, remember—"

"—Yes, I know," Theresa responded patiently. "Don't tell Maizie."

Nikki all but sang out the word, "Right," just before she ended the call. She was humming.

Theresa slowly closed her cell phone and then tucked

the pearl pink model back into her pocket. She raised her eyes and looked at the woman who'd dropped by for lunch less than ten minutes ago.

"Just so that you know," Theresa told one of her two oldest, dearest friends, "I'm not supposed to talk about what your daughter just said to me."

"Yes, I know." Maizie smiled the deep, satisfied smile of a mother whose plans were right on schedule. She'd been in Theresa's small, cozy office to overhear the entire call. It didn't take anything to put all the pieces together. "I wouldn't dream of having you tell me about the dinner you're making for my daughter to pass off as her own when she has Lucas Wingate over."

Theresa, the product of a strict upbringing, was the one whose conscience always made her chafe if she wasn't on the straight and narrow path. This came under the heading of deception. "You know, Maizie, I do feel rather guilty about this."

Maizie slipped a comforting arm around her friend's thin shoulders. A great deal of affection flowed between the two women.

"Don't be silly, Theresa. We're mothers. Being underhanded for our children's own good comes with the territory." Satisfied that she'd made her point, Maizie asked, "Now then, what are you going to make for my daughter's covert dinner? Remember," she cautioned, "nothing too elaborate. Nikki might not be able to answer him if he asks her what she'd 'made' and we don't want him knowing what a terrible cook she is until he's become enamored with some of her other excellent qualities."

Theresa merely smiled and shook her head. Maizie would have made a wonderful general if she'd joined the armed services.

Damn it, this was downright ridiculous.

Nikki could feel her heart accelerating. It was beating even faster than a couple of minutes ago. Going to answer the door was ratcheting up her heartbeat to a fierce level.

Theresa had left her house less than twenty minutes ago, placing everything she'd prepared on a warming tray she'd brought with her. Everything looked, and no doubt was, perfect. Theresa had even thought to bring along some newly made finger food for the baby so that, if nothing else, Heather would be occupied squeezing the food to a pulp.

Theresa had thought of everything. Too bad *she* couldn't think at all, Nikki thought. In comparison, molasses in January moved faster than her brain right now.

When she opened the door, admitting Lucas in, her heart all but stopped. He looked incredibly handsome in his deep blue shirt that matched the hue of his eyes, making them stand out and appear even more blue than they already were.

He also looked incredibly alone.

She was having trouble breathing. Very slowly, she drew in a long breath as subtly as she could.

"Where's Heather?" Nikki asked, opening the door wider as if that would somehow reveal where he'd hidden his daughter.

"Home," he told her, crossing the threshold. He handed her a bottle of wine he'd thought to bring at the last moment. "I thought maybe, since you have to deal with children all day long, you might want a baby-free dinner."

No. No, I don't.

Suddenly, jumbo jets flew inside her stomach, taking off and barely avoiding disastrous collisions. As long as Heather was present, the little girl provided a much-needed, diverse focal point. She was someone to talk about, someone who needed attention. Heather would have kept this whole dinner on a friendly, yet not quite personal level.

With the baby out of the equation, Nikki suddenly felt oddly vulnerable. And very nervous.

Because, she was forced to admit, she was more than just passingly attracted to the man in her doorway.

Lucas sniffed the air. "What smells so good?" he asked.

Nikki had to stop and think before answering. "Chicken divan."

"I'm impressed you went to so much trouble."

The first shaft of guilt found her. She turned away to lead the way into the living room.

"No trouble at all," she assured him a bit too breezily as she attempted to brush off the compliment. Doing her best to sound nonchalant, she asked, "You found a sitter?"

"Yes." He was very pleased about that accomplishment. "Turns out the person I called to ask for a referral was free and she said she'd be more than happy to babysit."

Placing the bottle of wine on the kitchen counter, Nikki took out a corkscrew. "And you trust her?"

Taking the corkscrew from her as if they'd been doing it this way for years, Lucas began to open the bottle. "Absolutely. She has one of those faces," he confided. "You know the type I mean. She's the kind of person you find yourself instinctively trusting and telling all sorts of things to that you wouldn't have thought you would ever share with anyone, much less someone you haven't known for years." He realized that he was looking directly at Nikki. And that, in her own way, she matched that description. "Kind of like you, actually."

Nikki stared at him, surprised and uncertain. "Me?"

Lucas nodded. Pulling out the cork, he set the corkscrew down and poured two glasses. He handed her the first one, then picked up his own. Lifting it, he silently toasted her before taking a sip.

"I think I've shared more with you than I have with anyone at the hospital where Heather was born. The hospital where…" Unable to finish the sentence, to summon Carole's death even verbally, he let his voice trail off.

Sensing what was going on, Nikki immediately changed the subject. "And Heather's comfortable with this sitter?" she asked.

"I think she likes her more than me," he laughed. "She took to the woman like a duck to water." And then, for a moment, he was serious. "I wouldn't have left her if she'd shown any signs of agitation."

Nikki believed him. She led the way back into the dining room. Perched on the warming tray, dinner was on the buffet against the far left wall, awaiting their pleasure.

"You know you really didn't have to leave Heather home," she told him. "I have little finger food for her to eat—or wear as the case may be. In any event, it would have kept her busy. Babies love to squish food between their fingers."

Lucas could just see Heather really getting into that—and leaving one hell of a mess behind. "Well, I did think you deserve not to feel as if you were literally bringing your work home with you. And, to be honest, I kind of needed the break myself. Except when I was house hunting, I haven't been away from her since we moved here."

She laughed, raising her glass in a mock toast. "Welcome to every at-home-mother's world."

"Personally," he told her, "I have a great deal of renewed admiration for moms. I always thought of them as incredible, but now I view them as somewhere in the realm of superhuman."

Setting down her glass next to her plate, Nikki brought over the large, covered dish that contained the chicken divan and set it on the table. The dish of rice followed.

"Being a mother is a juggling act," she agreed. "But the rewards are great."

Lucas surprised Nikki by drawing out her chair for her. "How is it that you don't have any children of your own?"

"Too busy taking care of everyone else's, I guess," Nikki answered. "Besides," she continued as he took his seat to her right, "the right man hasn't come along yet." The last words came out slowly as she found herself staring at him. The stray thought floated through her head that maybe she was looking at the right man.

The next moment, the thought vanished.

"We'd better eat," she urged, clearing her throat. If only her head was that easy to clear. "Dinner's liable to get cold."

He removed the lid from the larger dish. Steam rose. "Not much chance of that. You had it on a warming tray," he reminded her.

"Oh, well," She was tripping over her own tongue. "Warmed-over food isn't as good as when it first comes straight out of the oven. Which it did. A few minutes ago." She forced a smile to her lips as she instinctively shut them. Right now, the less she said, the better, Nikki decided.

Finished, Lucas leaned back in his chair. Lately, except for the meal he'd tried to make for Nikki, he'd just been eating to survive, grabbing anything he could and not paying too much attention to what he was consuming. But this time, he felt full, happily full. Two and a half servings full. He couldn't recall the last time that had happened.

"That had to be one of the best meals—no," he amended, "the *best* meal I've had in a very, very long time. And that's even taking my mother's cooking into consideration." Carole, bless her, knew which ready-made meals to get from the supermarket. She'd been a hell of a defroster. "Where did you learn to cook like that?"

Stymied, Nikki opened her mouth to brush off the compliment and act appropriately modest. But if she did, her words would all revolve around a lie. While she would, on occasion, resort to little white lies in order to spare someone's feelings or make them feel better, if she lied now it would only be self-serving. And the lie would only get bigger with time. Eventually, she was going to have to come clean—if there *was* an "eventually" in their future, she silently qualified.

"Actually," she confessed, forcing herself to meet his gaze, "I didn't."

"You didn't what?"

She was tempted to stare down at the napkin she was folding in her lap, but she forced herself to continue meeting his gaze. "I didn't learn to cook like that."

"I don't think I understand."

He was going to think she was really lame, Nikki thought, upbraiding herself for ever having gone this route to begin with.

"You're eating a meal prepared by one of my mother's best friends. Theresa, my mother's friend, is a caterer. There's a very strong suspicion that she's been cooking since birth. Personally, I can't boil water. Well,

I can," she amended, "but I usually wind up boiling it away and burning the pot." She shrugged in a self-deprecating manner. "I'm afraid I'm pretty hopeless in the kitchen when it goes beyond opening the refrigerator."

Amused by the expression on her face, and touched that she'd gone to all this trouble for him, Lucas did his best to keep a straight face. "Cooking's really no big deal."

He was just being kind and they both knew it. "It is if you can't."

He appreciated that she'd told him the truth, but he didn't want her beating herself up about this on his account. He wasn't here for the food, he admitted to himself, even though it was very good.

"I'm flattered that you felt you had to make such an effort for me," he began.

Nikki shrugged, self-conscious. She wasn't accustomed to feeling inept. Complicating things was the fact that he was being so understanding.

"Well, I couldn't exactly risk poisoning you now, could I?"

He laughed, dismissing her last words. "You couldn't be that bad."

She thought of her last foray into the culinary arts. Her mother, otherwise known as her biggest cheerleader, had almost choked on the dinner she'd *tried* to make. She'd made her promise never to cook for a prospective boyfriend until *after* the deal was sealed. "I wouldn't put me to the test if I were you."

Lucas reached over, covering her hand as he spoke. "Tell you what. Why don't we wipe the slate clean? Forget about my fiasco last week and forget about this excellent, catered meal, although my stomach may vote against that," he commented, then got back on track. "What do you say I take you out to dinner at a restaurant next time, so that we both can relax?"

There it went again, her heart upping its rate. His hand touching hers wasn't helping the situation any. *You're not supposed to get involved, remember?*

"I'm not sure about the relaxing part," she confessed quietly.

Feeling something electric telegraphing itself between them, Lucas withdrew his hand.

"You're right. But then on the other hand," he reconsidered, "maybe a little tension is a good thing."

Lucas raised the glass of wine to his lips, then stopped.

"Something wrong?" she asked.

He put the glass down on the table. "Well, if I finish this wine, I'm going to have to stay a couple of hours longer. I've only had one glass, but I wouldn't want to risk getting pulled over and wind up being charged with a DUI if I fail a breath test."

A safety net had suddenly materialized. This was where she agreed and got him to leave. But instead, she heard herself saying, "No one's ushering you out that I can see."

He smiled into her eyes, scrambling her already knotted stomach. "You talked me into it."

Mayday. Time to put distance between them at the very least.

"Nice to know I can be so persuasive." Nikki rose. She nodded at the glass in front of him. "Why don't you take that into the living room while I clear off the table?"

"I've got a better idea. Why don't you take *your* glass into the living room, Nikki, and *I'll* clear the table?"

She stopped picking up the dishes, placed the ones she had already gathered together on the table and shook her head. "All right, you have to stop that."

As far as he knew, he hadn't said anything offensive. "Stop what?"

"Stop being perfect."

He smiled broadly—and shyly. "Not so perfect, but I was trained well."

Since he'd brought it up, she felt it was safe to take a guess. "Your wife?"

"My mother," he corrected. "She always said that there was no shame in pitching in, that there was no such thing as 'woman's work' or 'man's work,' just 'family chores.'"

"I like your mother."

"Yeah, me too. My father didn't quite see things that way," he allowed, "but he was crazy about my mother so he went along with things—when he was home," Lucas allowed. His tone indicated that it wasn't all that often.

"He travel a lot?" she asked.

Now there was an understatement, Lucas thought.

"You could say that. My father was a Navy SEAL. He was gone for months at a time. When he came home, he'd play catch-up. By the time he was caught up, it was time for him to leave again. For the most part, my mother was the one who raised me."

And from what she could see, he turned out rather well. "Sounds like a special woman," she said as she picked up the plates again.

Lucas gathered up his own plate and placed it inside the large serving dish. There wasn't so much as a drop of food left.

"She was." He saw the hesitant question in her eyes. He answered before she could ask. "My mother died about five years ago."

He's certainly had more than his share of tragedy to bear, she thought, walking into the kitchen and placing the dishes on the counter beside the sink. "I'm sorry."

He thought of his father. The man had remained stoic throughout the funeral and its aftermath, but Lucas knew it hadn't been easy for him. His father wasn't made out of stone no matter how hard he tried to pretend he was. "Yeah, we all are."

The napkins she was holding slipped from her hands. Nikki quickly bent down to pick them up. And so did Lucas. They wound up bumping their heads, causing her to lose her balance.

She started falling backwards, but just before she wound up ignobly sitting on her rear, Lucas grabbed her arm to steady her. Rising up, he brought her to her feet along with him.

And just like that, Nikki found herself a little too close to him.

Again.

The moment froze.

Chapter Eleven

*B*reathe.

She had to remind herself to breathe. Breathe, not pant.

Every single promise Nikki had made to herself about not getting involved, about keeping her distance from Lucas, about not messing up what could possibly be a very nice friendship in the making went up in smoke just like that.

The heat of the moment burned those promises to a crisp.

And the moment *did* have heat. So much more than its rightful share. All of her felt ablaze with this wide, all-consuming desire. She couldn't say that it hadn't been there before, but certainly not like this. Not even close.

Although Nikki tried desperately to hide it, to suppress the feeling, she knew that there was hunger in her eyes, knew that he would see it unless she suddenly threw a paper bag over his head. Or hers.

Where was a frantic parent calling her answering service when she needed one? Her phones—her landline and her cell phone—remained dormant.

Her heart didn't. At this point, it raced more than a mile a minute.

The debate in Lucas's head went on for less than half of a heartbeat. He could do the right thing and step back. Or he could give in to a need that had emerged out of the shadows, taking him both by storm and by surprise.

There was just a twinge of guilt, the tiniest moment of indecision. He would have expected more, thought he would have agonized more, but all that had come before he'd ever felt this drawn to a woman. To Nikki.

The internal struggle didn't last long.

Lucas gave in.

The next moment, he released the arm he'd been holding and pulled Nikki even closer to him. Just before he pressed his lips against hers.

The kiss blossomed. The urgency grew, deepened, sweeping them both away.

The more he kissed her, the more he *had* to kiss her. The more he wanted to absorb her.

His heart slammed against his rib cage, threatening to break out. It didn't matter. Lucas could only keep on doing what he was doing. Losing himself in her in hopes of eventually finding his way out of this deep, long tunnel.

But not too quickly.

Not until he'd had his fill. Until this insatiable feeling clamoring within him was met and sated. At least to some degree. He was in no hurry for that to happen. Not until he explored this vast, endless new world he'd stumbled into and it took on a little more identifiable shape.

Nikki felt his strong, artistic hands gliding along her sides, caressing her. Molding her. Making her his without words being exchanged.

Surges within her threatened to short-circuit her very being.

Her hands shook a little as she struggled to quickly unbutton his shirt. Because they shook, it took her twice as long to do it. But finally, she finished and she yanked the shirt away from his shoulders, pulled it off his wide, muscular arms. She threw it God only knew where. She wasn't paying attention to something that insignificant. Her mouth still eagerly sealed to his, draining the very last bit of sustenance from it that she could, Nikki was already working on taking down his trousers.

That was when she realized that he was working his way through her clothes at the same time. Right now, as she'd flung away his shirt, he was pulling her sweater up, over her head. The next second, he cleared it from her arms.

All she wanted was for this feeling to continue a

little longer. Just a little longer. It had been forever since she'd felt like a desirable woman.

Nikki tried very hard not to attach any kind of importance to what happened between them, to the feelings singing inside her.

This was just sex, nothing more.

But his touch was so gentle even as she felt his urgency increase, that she all but melted into him, like whipped cream into an ice-cream sundae.

They did an awkward two-step, their lips sealed against one another, as they slowly made their way into the small family room and the sofa that was there. The journey from here to there was littered with fallen articles of clothing.

The more Lucas kissed her, the more Nikki prayed he'd never stop.

The more her body burned to be taken.

When they finally reached the sofa, their bodies were naked, ready, but Lucas still continued kissing her. Continued caressing her, making her heart jump in anticipation of what was to be.

His lips finally left hers, but not to undertake the final phase of this blazing pantomime they were caught up in. Instead, he kissed the hollow of her throat, the side of her neck. The creamy, inviting expanse above her breasts.

He made his way lower, lightly grazing each breast before suckling, creating a whole new world of fire and passions within her.

Nikki arched against his mouth as Lucas worked his

way down to her belly, creating mini earthquakes as he went. She was vaguely aware of digging her fingers into his shoulders, of holding him to her as his clever mouth caused explosions inside of her.

Until this evening, she'd thought that one lover was pretty much like another.

How could she have been so wrong?

Her inner core vibrated like a tuning fork and still Lucas continued playing her, arousing her. Making her crazy.

She tried, unsuccessfully, to muffle her cry when he suddenly made her climax. Failing, the sound echoed throughout the room as well as in her head. Gasping, Nikki fell back against the sofa, exhausted, only to have him start something agonizingly delicious all over again. She just didn't have the strength to endure it.

And then, she did.

Death by indescribable pleasure, Nikki thought. Imagine that. She was part of a pioneering step, a whole new way to kill someone.

After the second climax rattled her down to the very roots of her hair and to the bottom of her toes, she could barely catch her breath. But when she finally got back some semblance of it, Nikki was determined to bring Lucas to the brink of the precipice and then push him over, just as he had with her.

Dipping her hand below his waist, her eyes on his, Nikki gently closed her fingers over him, her thumb slowly stroking the length of him. Satisfaction wove through her as she noted that each pass of her fingers increased his passion. Increased his size.

And then, just when she was within seconds of triumph, Lucas was grabbing her hand, pulling her away. She looked at him, her eyes wide with an unspoken question.

Rather than say anything, he pressed her back against the sofa, drawing the length of his body slowly along hers. Bringing her to the very edge of yet another teeth-jarring climax.

This time, rather than tease and inflame, watching her face with a very solemn expression on his own, he entered her. After a beat drawn out so long she thought he would remain sealed within her forever, Lucas began to move. At first, he did so achingly slow. And then, an eternity later, his movements intensified. And kept on becoming more urgent in tempo until the stars rained down all around her, sealing her within an exquisite wall of fiery ecstasy.

She was never going to breathe right again, she thought. But it was a very small price to pay for feeling this way. And then, ever so slowly, the warm cocoon wrapped around her parted and receded. She wasn't ready for it to go yet. In an effort to freeze the moment, Nikki not only kept her arms around him but tightened her hold, as if that could somehow keep the rest of the world at bay. Could somehow keep the moment alive just a little longer.

To her surprise, rather than roll off her, or, in this

case, draw away and leave her the way Larry, her on-staff lover always did when they made love, Lucas framed her face and lightly kissed her lips.

It had to be the most tender moment she'd ever lived through. Her heart was a few breaths away from bursting.

And then, although the sofa was fairly narrow, Lucas moved so that he was tucked in beside her in the small space. His arms curved around her as he cradled her to him.

The next few moments, he knew, would be crucial. "Do I apologize for that?"

She stiffened reflexively. "You do and I'll be forced to cut your heart out."

She felt his chest ripple with a small echo of a chuckle. "Good."

Nikki struggled to rise up on her elbow and look down at him. "Good?" she repeated. Was Lucas a masochist who enjoyed diving into situations that were fraught with danger?

"Yes. Good. Because I don't want to apologize for what just happened." His lips barely touched her temple. But she felt the soft, fleeting imprint of a kiss. "I liked it too much to be sorry that it happened."

The smile came to her lips of its own accord. She didn't think there was any way she could suppress it. "Yeah, me, too." And then she raised her head again to look down at him. "I shouldn't have just admitted that, should I?"

"Can't really help you there," he admitted. "I've never been in this kind of situation before," he deadpanned. "Heather's last pediatrician was sixty-three years old and had a gray beard and sideburns."

Amusement rose into her eyes. "So you're not just a doctor groupie?"

His laugh was low and sexy and it immediately undulated under her skin, warming her.

"Nope, afraid not," he whispered softly into her hair. His fingertips stroked her hair ever so lightly. "You're the first woman I've slept with since…well, since," he ended, leaving it at that. Knowing that she would know.

It's not personal, don't take it too personally, she cautioned herself urgently.

"Are you considering this your coming-out party?" she asked.

"I'm not sure what I consider this," Lucas admitted truthfully. "Except, maybe, for damn confusing."

Struggling, Nikki did her best to sound as if she was in control of herself instead of in danger of melting like a vat of vanilla ice cream accidentally left out on the counter overnight.

"Regrets?"

"None," he answered firmly. And then he turned his head and looked at her as her question came back to him. "You?"

She saw no point in playing coy. "Only that it's over."

The smile that slowly unfurled on his lips was the last word in sensual. And tempting. "It doesn't have to be."

She grinned. "I could always make you drink another

glass of wine so that you'd have to stay for at least another hour, if not more."

Lucas touched her chin with the crook of his finger, sending fresh waves of desire through her. "I don't need wine to make me stay."

She could feel him wanting her again. Feel him hardening against her. Excitement vibrated through her limbs. The lovers she'd had, even the best of them, had all opted for sleep once the sex was over. The way Lucas felt against her told her that he was ready to go all over again.

Nikki watched him incredulously—and with admiration. "You're kidding."

"I might be smiling," he qualified, shifting so that he was over her again. "But I'm not kidding."

The delicious dance began all over again, and even though she knew—or thought she knew—what to expect this time, it wound up feeling like a wonderful surprise all over again. There were the same delightful surges, but somehow, they were new and different all the same.

This was not unlike being a child who had entered an amusement park by way of a different gate. The end destination would be the same, but the path to get there was not.

Delight waited for her at every turn. Delight, excitement and anticipation. They all scrambled within her.

It was all too incredible.

Lucas made her body sing.

And although she tried to turn the tables on him, tried to make Lucas feel as wildly enthusiastic as he made her, she only partially succeeded.

He was the master here, she willingly admitted, even as he made it all seem so effortless.

This time, she was fairly convinced, when they came together and made the rest of the world all but sizzle away into smoldering embers, that she would never breathe again. At least not evenly, without being conscious of making the effort.

Her heart hammered even harder this time around than the last.

Her only satisfaction—and it was a small one—was that, as she leaned her head against his chest, Nikki could hear his heart pounding just as hard, just as fast, as hers. The rhythm of Lucas's heart was strangely comforting. So comforting that she nearly dozed off without realizing it.

Coming to with a start, Nikki struggled to push herself upright. When she finally did, she looked down at his face. She'd hardly known him, yet he both excited her and, oddly enough, made her feel comfortable. The latter was more dangerous that the former.

She would have to be careful.

Otherwise, she could very easily find herself sliding into a relationship that wasn't there. It was all too wonderful to last. Right now, given the state of his life, he could be faithful only to one female. His daughter.

Even as she wanted just to remain like this and fall

asleep in his arms, she forced herself to murmur, "It's getting late."

Lucas raised his left wrist and angled it so that he could look at his watch.

When what he saw registered, he bolted upright. "Oh, God, you're right. It *is* late."

Lucas thought of the woman he'd left with Heather. She'd been so nice to him, he didn't want her feeling as if he'd taken advantage of her and the situation. That was no way to repay an act of kindness.

But God, he wanted to stay here, to feel things rather than just be going through the motions as one of the walking wounded.

Lucas took a deep breath, forcing himself to focus and not linger—even though everything tempted him to do the latter. "I'd better get home before Maizie thinks I've fallen off the face of the earth."

Nikki's heart stopped midbeat.

"Who?" Her voice was barely a whisper.

"Maizie," he repeated. She probably thought that was an odd name. Certainly not one you heard every day, he thought. "She's the one who volunteered to watch Heather." And then he realized that he'd made assumptions and had jumped ahead of himself. Nikki had no way of knowing who he was talking about. "Maizie was the woman who sold me my house. A really nice lady. You'd like her."

Mother, how *could* you? "I wouldn't make any bets if I were you."

He didn't seem to hear her. He was busy trying to remember something. "No, wait, I forgot. I think you know her."

She eyed him warily. If he'd known she was Maizie's daughter, wouldn't he have said something about that by now? "What makes you say that?" she asked cautiously.

"Well, for one thing, she's the woman who referred me to you."

She needed more input, Nikki thought. She'd be fair and hear everyone out. And *then* she'd strangle her mother. "Just like that?"

"Not exactly. After I signed the paperwork for my house, since she interacted with so many people, I asked Maizie if she knew a good pediatrician in the area. She told me she did and then she gave me your name and number," he told her.

"I see." She knew how her mother's mind worked. This was a setup. A round-about setup.

Okay, it *wasn't* his imagination. There was something strange about Nikki's voice. As if she was struggling to sound civil. He put getting dressed on hold for a moment and looked at her.

"What's the matter?"

For a moment, Nikki actually debated saying "Nothing," and pretending. But lies had a very bad habit of leading to more lies and even though she knew that, despite this temporary aberration, theirs was just a professional relationship. What kind of a doctor would he think she was if she lied to him about something like this?

Trying to brace herself for the consequences that loomed ahead, Nikki sat up. She pulled down the gray throw that normally made its home on the back of her sofa and tucked it around herself. She attempted to do more than just cover her nakedness. She felt far too exposed making this admission.

"Maizie is my mother."

Chapter Twelve

Nothing but silence met her disclosure for at least two beats.

And then Lucas rose from the sofa, gathered up his clothes and started to get dressed.

Nikki knew she was supposed to look away, but there was no arguing that the man who she'd just broken all the rules and made love with was an outstanding specimen of manhood. It took her several seconds, even in her present state of annoyed agitation, to force herself to shift her line of vision.

Was that amusement on his face? She blinked twice to clear up what she assumed was her foggy vision.

The expression remained unchanged.

Lucas slid on his slacks before finally responding to her declaration.

"You're kidding."

Those were not exactly the words she expected to hear. Nikki wrapped the gray throw more securely around her as she stood up herself.

"I wish I was, but, no, I'm not." Though simple, the admission was really difficult for her to push out of her mouth.

"Huh."

She stared at him, waiting for more. There wasn't any.

"That's it?" Nikki asked incredulously. "'Huh,'" she echoed, still waiting. She was absolutely stunned that there was no other display of emotion on his part. She had all she could do to bank down hers.

"Small world," Lucas marveled almost under his breath. Picking up his shirt, he pulled it on and began to button it up.

Another man, in her estimation, would have been angry, or at the very least, really annoyed. Annoyed that he'd been manipulated without his knowledge by a crafty woman who would, obviously, stop at nothing in her quest for a grandchild.

Yet he seemed utterly unfazed. Was that shock? Or did he think she was just kidding and was waiting for her to declare a theme and variation of "April Fool"?

"You're not angry?" she finally demanded. She peered at his face for some telltale sign to indicate what was going on in his head.

Being angry hadn't crossed Lucas's mind and now that she brought it up, he could only look at her in mild confusion.

"No, I'm not angry. Why should I be? Your mother must have had her reasons for not telling me that you were her daughter." An explanation occurred to him. "Maybe she thought that I wouldn't go to you if I knew that she was related to you."

Now he was making sense, Nikki thought. "I should say that—"

Tucking his shirt into his waistband, he continued with his thought. "She probably figured that I'd think she was prejudiced in her recommendation and I have to admit, I might have been. This way, I just assumed that she was referring me to the best pediatrician she knew." Adjusting his belt, he grinned at her. "Which is exactly what you turned out to be."

Lucas was getting it all wrong, she thought. Nikki held up her hand to stop him from going down this errant path. "Wait a minute. You don't feel that she *manipulated* you?"

"But she didn't," he protested. Why would Nikki even think that? "I asked for the name of a pediatrician and your mother gave me one. Yours as it turned out. I didn't have to go if I didn't want to. How is that being manipulated?"

Funny, he hadn't struck her as particularly innocent. Or naive. Nikki sighed. "You're missing the point. She set you up."

"Yes," he agreed, enunciating each word as if he was talking to someone who had trouble connecting the dots before her and deserved a little extra patience. "With a doctor for Heather. A doctor," he pointed out warmly, "who was selfless enough to put my daughter's well-being above her own comfort and come over when I called her in a total panic." He cocked his head, his eyes on hers. "How is that setting me up?"

Was he being dense?

Or was he just bent on seeing the positive in a situation rather than immediately ferreting out the negative? Maybe she should just quit while she was ahead. If Lucas didn't see it the way she did, she wasn't going to shine any more light on it for him.

"I'm sorry," she apologized, backtracking. "I guess I'm just used to seeing my mother from another perspective."

Lucas paused to put on his shoes, then turned to her and smiled. "You know, your mother really is a very nice lady."

When she's not butting into my life. Nikki suppressed a sigh. "She has her moments," she allowed.

"Mind if I ask you why you have different last names?" Had Nikki, like him, been married before, he suddenly wondered.

There was no big mystery, really. She was so used to it, it hadn't even occurred to her that someone else wouldn't know. No wonder he didn't make the connection, she realized. It wasn't Lucas's fault. It was her mother's. Again.

"Mother was always very independent. She went

back to selling real estate when I was five years old. Because she knew that my father's family wouldn't approve of his wife 'needing' to work—from what I gathered, Dad's parents were stuck somewhere in the late 1950s—Mother used her maiden name. 'Connors' was my dad's last name," she explained.

Lucas nodded his head. "Makes sense."

And that was it? Not even a drop of annoyance that he'd been fooled by the woman who'd sold him his house? "Just exactly how easygoing *are* you?" Nikki asked.

Lucas looked at her, his expression serious. "When the day your daughter's born turns out to be both the best day and the start of the worst day of your life, you wind up putting a lot of other things into perspective and not letting them get to you. My dad put it pretty succinctly when he told me, 'Don't sweat the small stuff. It's not worth your time.'"

She had a feeling that his father had a lot in common with hers. "Sounds like a pretty together guy."

Lucas nodded. "He is."

He needed to get going, Lucas thought, even though he really didn't want to. Slipping his arm around her waist, he drew Nikki close. He was struggling to bank down the very urgent temptation to pull the throw she'd wrapped around herself away.

For a second, he almost gave in.

But he knew that if he did, he wasn't going anywhere for at least another half hour. Maybe longer.

"I'd better get going," he repeated, as if that would

somehow propel his feet in the right direction. But he still didn't move.

"So you said," Nikki whispered.

She didn't want him to leave. *Really* didn't want him to leave. The feeling was so strong, it worried her. She didn't like having feelings this intense. It caused control to slip out of her hands. And without control, she would very possibly be setting herself up for another disastrous fall. She didn't exactly have a sterling track record when it came to men.

He needed to leave, she thought firmly, until she could sort all this out.

Nikki brushed her lips against his, then immediately took a step back so that she wouldn't be tempted to deepen the kiss. And get lost in it.

She wrapped her arms around the throw, which threatened to slip off. "Give her a hug for me," she instructed.

Lucas raised his brow. "Your mother?" Nikki hadn't sounded all that happy with the woman a moment ago.

"No, your daughter," she corrected. Right now, she had something else in mind for her mother and it didn't involve an embrace.

She walked him to the door. He stopped to linger a moment, wanting to hang on just a little longer to the feeling she was responsible for generating within him.

"I had a good time," he told her as he opened the door behind him.

"Me, too."

There was no reason to pretend otherwise. She'd all but laid bare her soul to him. He'd known she was lying if she seemed indifferent to their time together. Worse, he'd think she was playing games. She'd always loathed women—and men—who felt compelled to play games with one another instead of being honest.

Games like the ones the previous men in her life had played.

"Bye."

"Bye," she echoed.

Nikki noted, as she closed the door again and slowly emerged from the mental haze surrounding her brain, that Lucas had left without saying anything about getting together again. Realizing the omission caused her stomach to twist in a coarse knot.

Was he just in a hurry to get home and it was an oversight? Or had he deliberately not said anything because he wasn't interested in getting together again now that they had slept together?

Damn it, she wasn't going to do this to herself. Wasn't going to let this happen. Wasn't going to start making plans only to be brutally disappointed again.

This evening had just been about sex, she insisted not for the first time. *Sex.* Just cold, calculated, impartial sex, she emphasized silently.

"And don't forget it," she insisted out loud, addressing the words to the reflection she saw in the dark living room window.

Taking a long breath and then releasing it, Nikki

glanced at her wristwatch. Mentally, she added half an hour to the time she saw there. Thirty minutes was the amount of time she was going to give her mother to get home before she started calling.

Despite her plan, Nikki jumped the gun at twenty-five minutes. Pressing the single number that would instantly connect her to her mother's landline, she received no answer. She was too agitated to leave a message and terminated the connection.

Nikki kept calling her mother's number at five minute intervals, hanging up at the count of four rings. She tried for a total of four times before, finally, she heard the receiver being picked up.

She didn't even wait to hear her mother's voice before demanding, "How could you?"

Her mother took a fortifying breath on the other end of the line. "Hello, Nikki."

Nikki tightened her hand around her phone. "Don't 'hello' me."

Her mother sounded as if she was the personification of innocence. As if she had no idea what she'd done. "That is the proper thing to say when picking up a telephone, dear."

Nikki wasn't about to get sidetracked. "What did I tell you about interfering in my life?"

"Not to?" It wasn't really a question, but her mother framed it to sound like one. Well, she wasn't about to let her get away with it.

"Exactly. *Not to,*" Nikki emphasized. "So why did you?"

"But I didn't, dear," Maizie protested calmly. "What makes you think I did?"

For a second, Nikki was so stunned, she was almost speechless. Her mother should have been an actress, she thought. "You gave Lucas my name."

"Oh. That."

"Yes, 'that,'" Nikki ground out.

"Well, I had to."

"Had to?" Nikki demanded.

"Yes. The poor man was new out here. He was coping with everything on his own and he asked me for the name of a pediatrician for his daughter," her mother told her, sounding as if she was telling one of her numerous real estate stories. "Of course I gave him the name of the best one I knew. I am proud of you, dear. You really are an excellent pediatrician."

Nikki wasn't buying this innocent act. Her mother knew exactly what she was doing. She'd used the situation to set her up. To set them both up.

"If you were being so altruistic, Mother, why didn't you also tell the man that I was your daughter?" Nikki demanded.

"Very simple, dear," Maizie explained. "I was late for another showing. I'm afraid I didn't have time for chit-chat."

"Mother, you would make time to 'chit-chat' if the four Horsemen of the Apocalypse were galloping down your neck and it was three seconds before the end of the world."

Rather than become defensive, her mother laughed, clearly amused. "I don't know where you got this flair for exaggeration, Nikki. Your dear father, may he rest in peace, was such a down-to-earth man."

"I know where I got it from. Same place I got my hair color from. Originally," Nikki added since her mother, once a light blonde, had gone through several hair colors over the years. Just recently, she had settled on auburn. But that, like everything else, was just temporary.

"Your great-aunt Ruth?" Maizie guessed. Aunt Ruth had been the flamboyant member of the family before she died at the age of ninety-three two years ago. "You might have something there. But Aunt Ruth exaggerated because she couldn't remember the truth half the time."

Nikki closed her eyes, trying to summon strength. "You, Mom, I got it from you. Although, compared to you, I am a piker."

"Whatever you say, dear," her mother said in that singsong voice she used when she agreed merely to placate and not because she actually *did* agree. Nikki hated when she used that voice. She felt as if her mother was humoring her. "So, now that you feel as if you've 'unmasked' me, tell me, what do you think of Lucas?"

Oh no, Mother, I'm not getting sucked into your little trap. I give you any encouragement at all, you'll take it to mean you have carte blanche to set me up with every breathing, unattached male over the age of consent.

Out loud, Nikki said in a calm, disinterested voice, "He's an incredibly even-tempered man. He doesn't seem to mind being jerked around."

"Maybe that's because he doesn't think he was— which he wasn't." Maizie waited for her daughter to say something more. When she didn't, Maizie knew from experience that Nikki was angry. Maizie gave it another try. "I don't see why you're so upset. It's not as if I kidnapped you both and threw you on a deserted island to force you to interact with each other in order to survive the ordeal. Although—" she chuckled "—now that I say it out loud, it doesn't sound half—"

"Stop, Mother!" Nikki ordered uneasily. There was very little she would put past her mother once the woman got going. "Stop right there."

"Consider me stopped."

Nikki wasn't fooled. Her mother was using her humoring voice again. "Ha! If only."

Maizie decided to try to appeal to her daughter's common sense. Lucas Wingate was just too good a catch to throw back into the sea. Nikki *had* to be made to see that. She actually felt that the two needed each other. Lucas certainly seemed fine when he came home. He'd said that she should have given him a heads-up that Nikki was her daughter, but that it didn't change the fact that he'd had a good time.

Maizie took that to be a very good sign.

"Nicole, of the two of us, you are the more levelheaded one," she freely admitted. "Possibly boring, but definitely levelheaded. And this levelheadedness of yours has *got* to make you admit that I did nothing more than arrange circumstances which made it easy for the two of you to meet. I didn't make the child sick, I didn't even make Lucas call you. He was free to call any one of a number of hospitals in this region and ask them for a referral. He didn't. He turned to you. Because he trusts you."

"He wouldn't have even known about me if you hadn't initially sent him to me." Not that she was sorry things had turned out this way, but her mother could *not* be encouraged to keep doing this. "It's that earth-mother face of yours. It makes it hard to doubt you."

"Be that as it may—" Nikki could swear she heard a smile in her mother's voice "—the fact remains that all I did was give him your name. Whatever else happened or didn't happen is between the two of you. I had absolutely nothing to do with it. Scout's honor."

"You were never a Girl Scout, Mother."

"Don't nitpick, dear. It's not becoming. And for your information, I can still have their honor."

"Only if you stole it, Mother."

"Is that any way to talk to the woman who gave you life? And is responsible for bringing a very nice man into your life—nothing more, just bringing him in," she emphasized.

Nikki rolled her eyes. "You keep telling yourself that, Mom."

"I will, because it's the truth." And then her voice became more serious. "And why are you so angry about it?" There was a momentary pause and then her mother asked in a low, intuitive voice, "Is it because you like him? Is that why you're so angry with me? Because you're afraid that this is someone you could care about?"

"Mother—" Nikki suppressed the quick flare of anger she felt. There was a warning note in her voice, clearly intended to make her mother back away.

But Maizie wasn't the type to heed warnings, especially from her daughter. Doggedly, she pursued what she felt was her lead. "That's it, isn't it? You like him."

"He's a nice person," Nikki allowed. "But even so, I don't—"

"He's more than that," Maizie interrupted, pressing her advantage. "He was late coming home. He'd told me that he was going to be back before ten. It's almost midnight." The smile was practically radiating through the phone. "You had fun, didn't you, dear?" It was more of a statement than a question.

Denial wasn't going to get her anywhere. Once her mother had a notion in her head, it was impossible to shake it loose. Escape was the only answer. "I've got to go, Mother."

Why wouldn't Nikki let her guard down? When she'd been younger, they'd talked for hours, talking about the boys she liked, sharing feelings. Where had those times gone? Maizie lamented sadly.

"Nicole, there's nothing wrong with having fun. There's absolutely nothing wrong in letting yourself go a little. Even if you feel you made mistakes with your other choices, the odds are in your favor to finally make the right choice. Lucas Wingate could be that 'right' choice."

She never told her mother about Tony. Never told her how close she came to marrying him, only to discover that he was addicted to sex. Sex with every willing, breathing female who crossed his path.

She needed to think right now, not talk. Certainly not to be badgered. And then she heard a "beep" in the earpiece. The cavalry had arrived!

"I've got another call coming in, Mom. It's my answering service." She lied about the last part because she hadn't looked to see the identifying LCD display. Right now, she would have taken a call from a Riker's Island inmate.

"You've got another call coming in, all right. But it's not your answering service," Maizie told her knowingly. "It's your destiny."

This was getting her nowhere. Nikki stopped trying to talk her mother off the phone. Instead, she just broke the connection.

"Talk to you later, Mom." Pressing another button, she took the second call. "Dr. Connors."

"Did I remember to mention that I had a really nice time?"

The sound of Lucas's low, sexy voice warmed her all over, even as her mother's prophesy about destiny calling throbbed in her temples as she said, "Yes, you did. But I don't mind hearing it again."

"Good, because I'd like to see you again," he said, picking up on the word she used.

"When?" Did that sound too eager?

"Whenever you're free."

Both joy and fear ran at her from opposite ends of the spectrum. Reaching her at the same time, they wrapped themselves tightly around her.

This was good, she told herself. His wanting to see her again was good.

So why did her fingertips feel so icy?

Chapter Thirteen

There were times when Nikki felt as if she was inching her way across a pond covered with a thin sheet of ice, holding her breath as she tried to get from one end to the other while the early spring sun beat down on her. Any second, she expected to hear the ice cracking. To feel it opening up beneath her feet and then sending her plunging into the cold water just underneath. But even as she expected the worst, it—in this case her relationship with Lucas—held. Held firm as the days, then the weeks and finally the months slipped by.

Saying "months" made it sound longer than it actually was, she supposed. But technically, anything more than one qualified it to be thought of in the plural sense.

And she and Lucas *had* been seeing each other for almost six months now.

Six months and they were exactly in the same place as they had been that first time. *Exactly,* she thought, the word throbbing in her brain as she let herself into her house and hurried to get ready.

She'd actually planned on getting home early to give herself enough time to get ready slowly. To this end, she'd had Lisa reschedule her last appointment of the day. Jeremy Myers's mother was just bringing him in for a routine well-baby visit. That could very easily be put off until tomorrow morning without any problem and Edda Myers had been agreeable to the switch.

But just as she'd gotten into her car and turned the ignition, her answering service had buzzed her. One of her younger patients had had what wound up being an asthma attack—very scary for a young mother who had never witnessed one before.

Mrs. Wells was certain her three-year-old was going to die as she'd rushed him to the E.R. Heart in her throat, she'd frantically placed a call to Paul's pediatrician and had become almost hysterical when she got the answering service.

The service called her and just like that, the best laid plans of mice, men and pediatricians in love went awry.

Nikki had suppressed a sigh. "Call Mrs. Wells back. Tell her I'll be right there," she instructed and then drove the short distance to the hospital parking lot that was reserved for its MDs. She arrived there five minutes before Mrs. Wells and Paul did. It was almost textbook routine. Mrs. Wells left relieved and educated.

So now here she was, running late instead of early, hurrying and trying to stay one jump ahead of her thoughts.

But they still insisted on infiltrating, seeping into her head and making her question what should have been left alone.

Exactly.

The word rose up again to haunt her. Her relationship with Lucas was *exactly* the same as it had been last week and the week before that.

And the week before that.

Steadfast. Unchanged. No less and no more.

She knew she should be happy things were just the way they had been when they'd started sleeping together. She *knew* that.

And yet...

And yet, if everything was all right, shouldn't they be *going* somewhere? Progressing to another plateau?

Late at night, when she lay beside Lucas, waiting for her breathing to return to normal again, a tiny, tiny part of her kept wondering why there wasn't anything more on his end. Even though she tried to resist, she knew, *knew* that she was falling for him. *Really* falling for him. But she didn't get the sense that Lucas felt even an iota closer to her than he had in the beginning.

And he never talked about his wife.

Did that mean he was over her and moving on? Or did it mean that the mere mention of her name was too painful for him to bear? Was he carrying a torch for the woman? Was he comparing the two of them and finding that she came up short?

Oh, God, she wished she knew.

If she hadn't, early in the game, fallen for one charming, deceptive loser after another, she wouldn't be this nervous about parting with her heart.

"You're making yourself crazy," Nikki complained out loud.

Having swiftly changed out of her skirt and sweater into a stylish little black dress, she found that the strappy high heels she'd intended to wear weren't where they should have been.

"Terrific," she muttered. "Just what I need to calm me down. Lost shoes."

Nikki dropped to her knees and began pushing things aside on the floor of her closet, searching for the missing shoes. Painfully aware that time was short, she compromised and settled on another pair. She didn't have time to waste and she still wanted to check her makeup and fix her hair before Lucas arrived.

She was acting like a schoolgirl with her first serious crush, Nikki upbraided herself. She stopped combing her hair as the thought sank in. Well, in a way, she supposed that fit. She *was* acting like a schoolgirl. It had been a long while since she'd been willing to risk her heart.

And she was. It was out there, exposed, naked, for Lucas to pick up and cherish—or run over with his car.

Was she making a mistake? He seemed perfect, but

was he just too perfect to be true, she asked herself for quite possibly the hundredth time. Her mother would tell her that she should be happy and just enjoy what was happening without making any real plans, but that was just the problem. She was a making-plans type of woman. She knew that no matter how many times she told herself that it was wise to keep her distance emotionally, she kept whittling that distance down to nothing.

Being with Lucas had blown up the safe little haven she'd constructed for herself. He made her want what she'd been brought up to want: A home, a family. Somewhere, she felt certain, her mother was smiling.

"Obviously, you can take the girl away from the mother but you can't take the mother out of the girl." With a sigh, she put her lipstick down and leaned her forehead against the mirror. "What are you doing, Nikki? Are you willingly setting yourself up for a fall? Because if you are, this time it's going to be a doozy." She straightened again, picking up the mascara wand and applying another coat to her lashes. "This time you're falling from the top of the Empire State Building." Her lips twitched into a smile that had no humor behind it. "And not even King Kong was able to survive that, remember?"

The sound of the chimes had her quickly make one last pass at her lashes. Grabbing her shoes, she quickly headed for the stairs.

Nikki was almost halfway down before she realized that what she was hearing wasn't the doorbell. It was the telephone. She flew down the rest of the way and grabbed the first available phone.

"Hello?"

The calm, melodic voice belonging to Helen, the woman who had the evening shift at her answering service, greeted her warmly.

"Good evening, Dr. Connors. Emily Patterson asked that you meet her in the emergency room. She's rushing her daughter there. Janie was playing hide-and-seek in her girlfriend's yard. She tried to hide inside a rosemary bush, now she has a rash all over her arms and face and she's wheezing."

"This must be the day for allergies," Nikki murmured under her breath. *So much for dinner.* "Tell Mrs. Patterson that I'm leaving from my house, Helen. I'll be at the hospital as soon as possible."

"Yes, Doctor," Helen replied. A moment later, she ended the call.

Nikki dropped the portable receiver back into the cradle. The second it made contact, there were more chimes. But this time it really was the doorbell.

I'm going to have to turn him down. Maybe this is just as well, Nikki thought, hurrying to the door. Maybe, since Lucas wasn't moving forward, she needed to take a step back and evaluate everything from a different perspective.

Nikki pulled open the door. Her breath caught in her throat.

The man had to be taking "handsome" pills. There

was no other explanation why he just kept getting better looking each time she saw him. He was wearing a navy jacket, a light blue shirt and light gray slacks. Nothing spectacular, at least, not on another man. On him it seemed incredible.

"What's wrong?" he asked the moment she opened the door and he looked at her.

Assuming that something was wrong with her apparel, she looked down at herself. "Why? Did I put my dress on backwards?"

"No," he corrected, "You put your expression on backwards." When she looked at him, puzzled, he explained, "You're frowning."

She was going to have to get better at keeping a poker face, Nikki chided herself. "I'm going to have to cancel our date."

"Oh. Any particular reason?"

He sounded unfazed by what she'd just said. As if it was all one and the same to him. She *was* right. He didn't really care.

Banking down her feelings, she answered his question trying to sound as detached as possible. "My answering service just called. One of my patients is having an allergic reaction to rosemary."

Curious, Lucas asked, "The seasoning, or is that a person?"

"Neither. She had an allergic reaction to a rosemary bush from what I gather." She picked up her purse. She'd just transferred her wallet and keys into the clutch bag. It seemed inappropriate for a hospital, but she didn't have time to switch back. "I'm meeting the girl and her distraught mother in the E.R."

He nodded, stepping back as she crossed the threshold. "Is it serious?"

Quickly locking up, she turned to look at him. "I don't know. I won't know until I get there." She pressed her lips together, debating apologizing. After all, he didn't exactly look disappointed by this turn of events. In the end, she decided to make a token apology. "I'm sorry."

Lucas waved away her words. "Can't be helped." He walked her to her car, then waited as she unlocked it. He held the door open for her. "I'll call you."

Nikki forced a smile to her lips and just nodded in response as she got in behind the steering wheel of her car. A second later, she was pulling away.

The least he could have done was look disappointed. At least a little bit. It wouldn't have cost him anything to fake it. But it looked as if it didn't matter to him one way or another if she broke their date. Maybe she was just a place holder. Good enough to pass the time with until something better came along.

There was an ache in the center of her chest. In her heart.

Think about it later, Nikki. You need to be a doctor right now, not some paranoid, lovesick woman.

Biting down on her lower lip, making her mind as much of a blank as she could, Nikki floored the car as she drove on to the freeway on-ramp.

* * *

"I don't know how to thank you for coming," Emily Patterson said for the third time in twenty minutes, hovering over her daughter as she watched every move that Janie's pediatrician made.

Nikki smiled at the little girl lying on the cot. Janie's sobs and screams had finally subsided, thanks to the injection she'd administered fifteen minutes ago. The rash on both of Janie's arms and on her neck was no longer an angry red, more like a blushing pink that even now, was fading away.

"I want you to promise me that you won't play any more hide-and-seek inside bushes you don't recognize. Better yet, no more bushes at all." She stroked the little girl's golden-blond hair. "Okay, kiddo?"

"Okay," Janie promised. There were dried tracks of tears on her face.

As Nikki turned away from the gurney, Emily Patterson drew her aside. She made no attempt to hide the concern on her face.

"Should I be worried, Dr. Connors?"

In Nikki's opinion, Mrs. Patterson was *always* worried and always anticipating the worst. It made her grateful that she'd had the mother she had. Despite the fact that there were times her mother drove her crazy, she had to hand it to Maizie Sommers. She'd always given her enough freedom to stretch and grow.

"No," Nikki advised. "Just be careful. Read the labels on any boxes or cans of prepared food." She could see by Mrs. Patterson's puzzled expression that the woman wasn't following her. "If one of the ingredients mentioned is rosemary, I'd suggest skipping it unless you want a repeat performance of this afternoon."

Janie's mother looked horrified at the mere suggestion. "Oh, God, no."

Nikki removed the small piece of paper from the clipboard that held all of Janie's information. The top paper contained the prescription that she'd written for the little girl.

"Here, fill this at the hospital pharmacy—it's in the basement right by the elevator," Nikki told her. "And then you're good to go."

Mrs. Patterson folded the slip and tucked it into her purse. "Thank you." Tears glistened in the woman's eyes. Nikki sincerely hoped the woman learned how to relax before Janie became a teenager. "Thank you," Mrs. Patterson repeated, squeezing her hand.

Nikki nodded. She winked at Janie, then said to Mrs. Patterson, "You're welcome."

The woman's eyes swept over Nikki's black dress. "And I'm sorry I took you away from your evening," she apologized.

Nikki almost asked her how she'd known, then remembered that she wasn't exactly dressed the way she usually was.

"That's all right," she assured Janie's mother. "I'm just glad we could resolve this so quickly. You were very brave, Janie," she added.

Janie beamed.

Pausing to sign the little girl's paperwork which officially released her, Nikki handed over the clipboard to a nearby nurse. "She's ready to go once her mother picks up her medicine."

With that, Nikki headed for the rear of the large room. She walked out through the electronic doors the paramedics used when they brought patients into the ER. Evening was in full bloom. A large amount of stars were woven through the sky.

It was a night made for lovers, she thought with a pang.

As if to remind her of the detour her evening had taken, her stomach rumbled. She realized she hadn't eaten yet.

Out of the corner of her eye she caught a movement in the tiny parking lot reserved for E.R. patients. Someone was either coming or going. Hopefully, it wasn't another one of her patients. She felt drained. And yet, she was really wired as well. The wired part had nothing to do with Janie and her sudden allergic reaction to rosemary.

Lucas was responsible for that feeling.

She debated calling him, then decided against it. She didn't want to appear needy.

Maybe she'd stop at a drive-through and get a hamburger and fries. Not particularly healthy but at least it would be fast.

Lost in thought, Nikki didn't hear or see the man approaching her until he was directly beside her.

"Finished?"

Taken completely by surprise, Nikki's head snapped around. The second she saw him, her mouth dropped opened.

Lucas.

"What are you doing here?"

Lucas smiled at her. He liked the fact that her face was so expressive. Liked a lot of things about her. "Waiting for you."

He hadn't said anything about waiting when they'd parted in her driveway. If she'd known, she would have told the lab to hurry the tests through.

"All this time?"

Lucas glanced at his watch. "It wasn't that long," he responded. "Besides, I think I worked out the glitch in the new software program I've been developing."

He didn't add that the program had been commissioned by a branch of Homeland Security, the nature of which he wasn't at liberty to discuss. His father had connected them, something else he wasn't free to mention.

Nikki looked at him, stunned. "Seriously?"

He raised a shoulder in a half shrug. "Well, I'd have to go home and put it to the test, but yes, I think I might have actually solved it."

Nikki shook her head. "No, I mean seriously? You've been here the entire time, waiting for me to come out of the hospital?"

He would have willingly waited twice as long for her, but all he said was, "Yes."

He struck her as a very intelligent man. But his

actions weren't logical. "But I could have come out through any of the other doors."

He pointed to the light blue Toyota parked to the extreme left of the lot, directly against the wall. "Your car's here. I figured you weren't going to walk home. If you're too tired to go to the restaurant, we can always get dinner to go," he suggested. Her stomach picked that moment to growl again. "I'll take that as a yes."

Nikki was too tired to be embarrassed about the noises coming from her stomach. She nodded. "That would be nice."

He ran his thumb along her cheek. "How about if I drive you over to my house and then bring you back here to pick up your car tomorrow morning?"

She shook her head. "No, I'm okay. I can drive, and besides it's not that far to your place."

"All right, I'll follow you."

"Why?"

"To make sure you don't drive off the road—or a ramp," he added for good measure. "Once we reach my place, I'll call in the order then go pick it up. The extra time will allow them to fill the order and have it ready when I get there."

He'd thought of everything. Nikki nodded. "Sounds like a plan." And she could use the extra time to make herself presentable. "Tell me, how long were you planning on staying out here and waiting?"

"Until you showed up." He anticipated her next question. "I have a very understanding babysitter," he deadpanned. "She seems to have a vested interest in our seeing each other."

Nikki groaned. *Please don't have said anything to embarrass me, Mother.* "What did she say to you?"

"Nothing specific," he answered. "Maizie just told me that I could call on her anytime. She loves babysitting for Heather. Your mother and Heather get along very well."

"My mother likes children." If anything, that was an understatement. He held the door open for her and she slid in behind the steering wheel. "She especially likes the ones who are too young to talk back."

Lucas laughed. "There is something to be said for that. I'll meet you at the house," he told her, then closed her door.

She watched him as he hurried back to his own vehicle.

The thought that he was one in a million crossed her mind. The next moment, she remembered that her mother had once described her father that way. Just shortly before he died.

Happiness was not meant to last a lifetime. But for however long it lasted, she decided that she should stop dissecting the anatomy of their relationship and just enjoy it.

If only she could stop anticipating the end.

Chapter Fourteen

The restless disquiet refused to abandon her.

Like a hitchhiker who had managed to hide himself inside one of the freight train cars, Nikki's small, budding fear had climbed aboard and folded itself into the shadows. Growing larger and more unmanageable with each day that passed.

Her fear revolved around the same thing. That she was falling for this man and that he didn't return the sentiment.

"He doesn't talk about the future, at least not *our* future," Nikki told Kate as she frowned down at the designer-styled container of coffee she'd agreed to grab with her friend.

Once a month, she and Kate Manetti, Theresa's

daughter, along with Jewel Parnell, Cecilia's daughter, tried their best to get together and catch up on each other's lives.

It didn't always work out. This time around, for one reason or another, three and a half months had gone by since they'd last gotten together. In addition, Jewel had had to beg off, saying she was so busy, she had to schedule being able to draw more than two breaths in a row. She'd told Nikki to e-mail her. Nikki knew how that went. They'd wind up seeing each other before Jewel got around to reading her e-mail.

But one friendly ear was better than none.

"Lucas talks about his daughter's future and his plans for her, but he never says a word about any plans he might have for us." Placing her container down on the tiny round table inside the café, Nikki paused and looked at Kate. Waiting.

Taking another sip, Kate's eyes met her friend's. "You're waiting for me to comment?" she guessed.

"Well, yes, that's the general idea." Like their mothers, the three women had grown up together. They shared things with one another they wouldn't have dreamed sharing with their mothers. "What do you think it means? Or doesn't mean?" Nikki threw in. She needed a fresh pair of eyes, someone to guide her, to tell her if she was missing something or expecting too much. "Am I just some placeholder for him? Someone to hang out with until he gets his life straightened out?"

Kate was a lawyer. A good lawyer. And she knew

her way around words very well. But Nikki was her friend and she wasn't about to try to be glib or snow her. Nikki deserved the truth, the whole truth and nothing but the truth.

"Honey, I'm the last person in the world to give out romantic advice. The couple of times I was at bat, I struck out." Kate paused to take another sip of her coffee. "Now they won't even let me into the dugout."

Nikki stared at the dark-haired young woman, stunned. "Baseball metaphors? I'm asking you for advice and you're giving me baseball metaphors?"

Kate flashed a semiapologetic smile. "Sorry, it's spring. You know how Kullen gets every spring," she said, referring to her older brother. And then she grinned. "He's an optimist at heart—who knew? He keeps hoping the Angels will win another pennant. When he's not in court or with a client, my brother wanders around the office, babbling about stats and long shots with anyone who has ears.

"But the metaphor stands," Kate insisted. "I don't have any real words of wisdom to pass on to you, Nik, except to say: Go with your gut."

That was part of the problem. "My gut's all tied up, Kate." Rather than drink her coffee, Nikki toyed with it. "It's not going anywhere."

Kate raised her eyebrows, then leaned forward. "I'm no expert—"

Nikki didn't want disclaimers, she wanted help. "We've already established that."

Kate continued as if she hadn't been impatiently interrupted, "But if your stomach's all tied up, it must be because you like him."

Well, duh.

Nikki frowned again. "So far, you're not sounding like someone who graduated at the top of her class from law school. Of course I like him. The problem is: *am* I just spinning my wheels, getting more and more entrenched in the mire by the minute?"

Kate inclined her head, waiting for more. "And if you are?"

Nikki didn't know what her friend was getting at. "What's that supposed to mean?"

"If you are 'just spinning your wheels and getting entrenched' in a single spot, what does that mean to you?" She saw that Nikki still didn't understand. "Do you want to cut bait and run, or hang around until this single father of the year comes to his senses and realizes that you're indispensable?"

That was exactly what she was agonizing over. "What if he *never* gets to that point, never finds me indispensable?"

Kate took a breath, thinking. "If you like this guy as much as you say you do and nothing comes of this, you haven't lost anything, just gotten some nice one-on-one time with him."

That was settling for crumbs, Nikki thought. "I don't want to just settle, Kate." She shook her head, rejecting the idea. "That seems so needy."

Kate swung in the opposite direction. "Then break it off, Nik. That's what you were thinking of doing, wasn't it?"

"Yes," Nikki admitted reluctantly.

"Okay, then do it," Kate advised. "Maybe this father of the year's one of those guys you have to light a fire under before he finally acts."

Nikki knew that it would be the only way to finally see if there was any real hope for the two of them. But part of her was hesitant to push him. Because he might not react the way she wanted him to.

"And if he's not one of those guys?" Nikki asked. "If lighting a fire under him *doesn't* make him move? Then what?"

Kate was brutally honest. "Then you had a nice time, but it was going to end anyway. Might as well be on your terms and not his." She glanced at her watch and suddenly popped up to her feet like an expensively dressed jack-in-the-box. "I'm due in court in fifteen minutes. We've got to do this more often." She picked up her briefcase. "Great seeing you, Nik."

"Yeah, you, too."

But Nikki was saying the words to Kate's back as her lifelong friend moved swiftly through the café to get to the exit.

Somewhere in the twenty minutes that it took her to get back to her office, Nikki made up her mind. Kate was right, although the woman probably didn't even realize how right she was. There was only one way to handle this situation she found herself in.

Only one way to be prepared.

She had to make the first move. Call this off before Lucas dropped his own bombshell and walked away.

Entering her office—eerily quiet without the usual collection of small- and medium-sized patients, thanks to the fact that it was the tail end of lunchtime—Nikki went straight to her office. Her computer was on the way it always was during the day—it had been running twice as efficiently, not to mention quickly, since Lucas had overhauled it.

She tried not to think about that as she opened up the application that listed all the different doctors who were associated with Blair Memorial Hospital. Nikki "flipped" through the various virtual pages until she found the one she was looking for.

Allan Crosby.

She was going to have to refer Lucas and his daughter to another doctor. Allan Cosby was an excellent pediatrician and she was confident that the man would provide the little girl with the kind of care she needed and deserved. With Heather's health in good hands, there was no reason for Lucas and her to see one another anymore.

Unless he made it clear that he wanted to.

She could feel a lump in her throat and forced herself to ignore it. Instead, she focused on the fact she didn't want to set herself up for the inevitable fall that she knew in her heart was coming. She really wished she didn't believe that, but what other conclusion could she draw? Lucas hadn't given *any* indication that he wanted anything more from the relationship. What they had right now were hot nights and warm takeout.

Maybe that was enough for him, but it wasn't for her. She didn't want to *replace* his wife. What she wanted was for him to give her some kind of sign that he wanted her to someday *be* his wife. Different than the first, but with good qualities nonetheless. Good qualities that he cherished.

She could spend the rest of her life waiting, but it wasn't going to happen.

Waiting for some kind of positive sign ate at her. She needed to end it before her heart was ripped out of her chest.

This was the right thing to do, she silently insisted as she printed out Crosby's address and phone number.

If it was so right, why did it feel so wrong?

The lump in her throat grew bigger.

"What are you in the mood for tonight?" Lucas asked as he opened the door a second after Nikki rang the bell. "Chinese? Pizza?"

Lucas looked at her as if he knew something was wrong. As if he could feel it. Did he have any idea how she felt? She wasn't smiling and she wasn't coming in. Instead, she'd only taken a step inside the house, trying to act like a disinterested messenger.

"I'm not staying."

Instead of feeling a weight falling off her shoulders, Nikki felt as if each word she uttered weighed a ton.

"Another emergency?" he guessed. "You could come over after you finish dealing with whatever it is you're dealing with. I'll wait up for you," he offered.

This was the hardest of all to say. "I'm not coming back."

"Oh?"

Oh. No emotion, no demands to know why. No plea that she change her mind. Just a single, small word, as if he was surprised by a contestant's answer to an obscure game-show question.

She was right, Nikki thought, her stomach sinking down to her knees. He really didn't care. So she pushed on, holding out the piece of paper she'd printed. "I brought you the name of a good—no, an *excellent* pediatrician."

He didn't move to take it from her. "And why would I need this? I have you."

"No, you don't." Her mouth was so dry, the words almost stuck to the roof of her mouth.

"Oh?" His voice was low, still. "And why is that?"

Lucas sounded so calm, so unfazed. Secretly, she'd really been hoping that he'd raise his voice, that he'd shout, demanding to know what was going on. Instead, he sounded completely complacent.

Damn him.

Why can't you feel about me the way that I feel about you?

"It's just not working," she finally said. "And that's all right. I understand."

"You do?" Not once did he break eye contact with her. It was unnerving.

"Yes." Every second was now torture for her. She just wanted to go, to flee, not stand here talking, pretending her heart wasn't breaking. "But under the circumstances, I think it's best for everyone, especially Heather, if you took her to another doctor." She pushed the paper into his hand.

Lucas looked down at it. "And this Dr. Crosby—"

"Is terrific. I'll forward Heather's file to him in the morning." She hadn't done it already because some small part of her had gone on hoping against hope that he would say something to make her think she'd imagined things. That she'd made a mistake.

She needed to go. Now, before she cried.

"Take care of yourself, Lucas." She wanted to kiss him one last time, but she didn't trust herself. She wouldn't leave if she kissed him.

Nikki quickly turned on her heel and fled.

Leaving Lucas to stare at the paper in his hand. Finally, he turned toward Heather who was lying in the port-a-crib, kicking her legs.

"What just happened here, Heather?" he asked. "Do you have any idea at all? Because I sure don't."

His daughter made no answer. She just went on tap-dancing in the air.

From the moment she left Lucas's door, Nikki made sure that every single moment of her day was accounted for and stuffed to the gills with work.

Even so, she'd never known the days to drag by so slowly. Eighteen days had gone by since she'd walked out of Lucas's house. Eighteen days and he hadn't called her, hadn't tried to get back in contact with her, not even once.

She'd been right. Damn him.

Being right had never felt so awful.

She ran her hand over her forehead. She could feel another headache taking hold. Lately, she'd had more than her share. It was Friday afternoon. The prospect of the weekend loomed over her like a dark threat. She'd upped her volunteer work since she'd broken it off with Lucas, but none of the places needed her this weekend.

That meant she'd have time on her hands. She didn't want time. Because time meant that she could think. And regret.

There was a quick rap on her door and Bob stuck his head in. "One last patient, Dr. C," he announced.

Nikki pushed herself away from her desk and rose to her feet. She must have missed that one. When she'd walked down the hall to her office after seeing Jason Jessop for his booster shot, she'd thought she was finished. There'd been no folders waiting for her to peruse.

"Room 5." Bob pointed toward the closed door. "Mind if I leave early? I want to get a jump-start on the weekend."

I'd gladly give you mine.

The other nurse had left half an hour ago. Something about going away for the weekend. Nikki usually liked to have one nurse on the premises when she saw a patient in case she needed help.

"Is Room 5 a routine visit?" Nikki asked the nurse.

"It's a follow-up," he said evasively.

Ordinarily, Bob handed her a folder, or left it tucked in the slot in the door. This time, he did neither. She looked at him quizzically. "Where's the file?"

His dark eyebrows rose high on his forehead. "Oh, I must have left the file inside the room." His lips pulled into an embarrassed smile. "My bad."

She waved her hand at his assumption of guilt. "Never mind, no harm done. Who is it?" she asked.

When there was no answer, she turned around. Only to find that Bob had disappeared around the corner in the hall. Presumably he'd gone back to the front of the office.

What had gotten into him?

He was anxious to start his weekend, that's what, she told herself.

Nikki sighed heavily. Lately, she'd been doing a lot of that, she thought. Putting her hand on Room 5's doorknob, she twisted it, opened the door and walked in.

Then stopped dead.

"Lucas!" Her first inclination was to throw her arms around him, but that would only propel her back to square one. So she held her ground. "What are you doing here? And where's the baby?"

He'd missed her a great deal, but the actual full extent didn't hit him until just this minute. It felt as if his very soul lit up. He'd been so afraid to let himself go, to let himself love again. But he realized now that he had no control over something like that. Not when it was real. When he'd lost Carole, he was certain he'd never recover, never love again. To find out that he could felt like a humbling miracle.

"She's fine." He didn't tell her that he'd left Heather with her mother who had been more than happy to watch the child. "We have to talk," he told her.

Tension wove through her. "I thought we already did."

"No, *you* talked," he corrected. "I listened. Now it's my turn to talk and your turn to listen."

She didn't want to listen because her resolve would fall apart. Even if he only recited the alphabet. If he said the slightest kind thing, it would be all over for her.

Still, she couldn't just throw him out, either. "All right."

"To begin with, Heather doesn't like Dr. Crosby. She bursts into tears when she sees him."

Disappointment rushed in. Was that what this was about? He was here to get another referral?

Well, what do you expect? You all but gave him the bum's rush. You hurt his ego.

"All right," she said quietly, turning to the door. "I'll refer you to someone else."

Lucas shifted and blocked her path. "No, you won't," he informed her. "She doesn't want to be referred to anyone else. She wants you."

She was losing ground. Nikki couldn't suppress the

amused smile that came to her lips. "Heather's gotten pretty vocal since I last saw her."

"Someone told me that they do a lot of growing in the first year," he deadpanned. And then he grew serious. Taking her hand in his, Lucas looked into her eyes. "What did I do wrong, Nikki?"

"Wrong?" she echoed.

"Yes, 'wrong,'" he repeated. He forced back a wave of frustration. "I had to have done something wrong for you just to walk out on Heather and me like that."

She skirted the answer. "I walked out to make it easy on you. And me."

He didn't follow her. He'd given her time and space, but she hadn't come back. He'd gone over and over the situation and came up with no answers. At this point, he needed a clue.

"Make *what* easy?"

"The breakup that was coming." She closed her eyes and sighed. That sounded really silly out loud. She broke up with him to prevent a breakup. He'd never begin to understand that.

She was right.

"The only breakup that was coming was the one you initiated," Lucas pointed out. "Up until then, I thought things were going pretty well—and then you dropped that little bomb on me."

Maybe they were going "pretty well" in his eyes, but they weren't going anywhere in hers. That was the problem. She could only make judgments about things by the input she'd gotten.

"I didn't think it mattered to you one way or another," she said, referring to the breakup. "I didn't think that I mattered."

Lucas stared at her. She was making less and less sense to him. "How could you possibly think you didn't matter?"

"How could I not?" she countered, pulling her hand away. "You never talked about our future together, never said anything about how you felt about me, or even *if* you felt anything at all."

He looked like Newton at the moment the apple had fallen on his head and he'd discovered the theory of gravity. "You're kidding. Is that it? Damn."

For a second, it looked as if he was internalizing an argument. But then the next moment, he grabbed her by the arms, pulling her close to him, as if that would help communication between them.

"I didn't say anything because I didn't want to scare you off. I was afraid that you'd think you were only getting me on the rebound. I was deliberately *trying* to go slow so that you would know that what was happening between us was real. That it wasn't happening because I was trying to replace Carole with the first beautiful, warm, sensitive woman who came along."

Her eyes widened as the words sank in. Things began to fall into place. It was all making sense now. "Really?"

"Really," he underscored. Well, he'd come this far, he might as well tell her everything. "I know it's too soon to ask you to marry me, but I would like you to give 'us' another chance. I want to be part of your life, Nikki, and I want you to be part of mine—Heather's and mine—for all the tomorrows that we have."

Her eyes met his. "No."

"No?" he repeated incredulously. He'd just bared his soul and she was turning him down?

"No." This time, she accompanied the word with a nod of her head, as if confirming her answer. "No, it's not too soon for you to ask me to marry you. And if you don't want to ask me, then I'll ask you. Lucas Wingate, will you mar—"

The laugh interrupted her.

She didn't get a second chance to finish her question. Moving her lips proved to be too difficult when another set of lips were pressed against them.

But that was all right. She had her answer.

They both did.

* * * * *

Don't miss Marie Ferrarella's next romance in May 2010 from Silhouette Romance Suspense!

Harlequin offers a romance for every mood!
See below for a sneak peek from our paranormal
romance line, Silhouette® Nocturne™.
Enjoy a preview of REUNION by USA TODAY
bestselling author Lindsay McKenna.

Aella closed her eyes and sensed a distinct shift, like movement from the world around her to the unseen world.

She opened her eyes. And had a slight shock at the man standing ten feet away. He wasn't just any man. Her heart leaped and pounded. He reminded her of a fierce warrior from an ancient civilization. Incan? She wasn't sure but she felt his deep power and masculinity.

I'm Aella. Are you the guardian of this sacred site? she asked, hoping her telepathy was strong.

Fox's entire body soared with joy. Fox struggled to put his personal pleasure aside.

Greetings, Aella. I'm the assistant guardian to this sacred area. You may call me Fox. How can I be of service to you, Aella? he asked.

I'm searching for a green sphere. A legend says that the Emperor Pachacuti had seven emerald spheres created for the Emerald Key necklace. He had seven of his priestesses and priests travel the world to hide these spheres from evil forces. It is said that when all seven spheres are found, restrung and worn, that Light will return to the Earth. The fourth sphere is here, at your sacred site. Are you aware of it? Aella held her breath. She loved looking at him, especially his sensual mouth. The desire to kiss him came out of nowhere.

Fox was stunned by the request. *I know of the Emerald Key necklace because I served the emperor at the time it was created. However, I did not realize that one of the spheres is here.*

Aella felt sad. Why? Every time she looked at Fox, her heart felt as if it would tear out of her chest. *May I stay in touch with you as I work with this site?* she asked.

Of course. Fox wanted nothing more than to be here with her. To absorb her ephemeral beauty and hear her speak once more.

Aella's spirit lifted. What *was* this strange connection between them? Her curiosity was strong, but she had more pressing matters. In the next few days, Aella knew her life would change forever. How, she had no idea....

*Look for REUNION
by* USA TODAY *bestselling author
Lindsay McKenna,
available April 2010, only from
Silhouette® Nocturne™.*

Copyright © 2009 by Lindsay McKenna

HARLEQUIN®

INTRIGUE®

WILL THIS REUNITED FAMILY
BE STRONG ENOUGH TO EXPOSE
A LURKING KILLER?

FIND OUT IN THIS ALL-NEW
THRILLING TRILOGY FROM TOP
HARLEQUIN INTRIGUE AUTHOR

B.J. DANIELS

WHITEHORSE MONTANA

Winchester Ranch

GUN-SHY BRIDE—*April 2010*

HITCHED—*May 2010*

TWELVE-GAUGE GUARDIAN—
June 2010

www.eHarlequin.com

HI69465

Silhouette®

SPECIAL EDITION

INTRODUCING A BRAND-NEW MINISERIES FROM *USA TODAY* BESTSELLING AUTHOR

KASEY MICHAELS

SECOND-CHANCE BRIDAL

At twenty-eight, widowed single mother Elizabeth Carstairs thinks she's left love behind forever....until she meets Will Hollingsbrook. Her sons' new baseball coach is the handsomest man she's ever seen—and the more time they spend together, the more undeniable the connection between them. But can Elizabeth leave the past behind and open her heart to a second chance at love?

FIND OUT IN

SUDDENLY A BRIDE

*Available in April
wherever books are sold.*

Visit Silhouette Books at www.eHarlequin.com

SSE65517

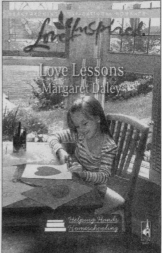

Love Inspired®

Single father Ian Ferguson's daughter is finally coming out of her shell thanks to the twenty-three-year-old tutor Alexa Michaels. Although Alexa is young—and too pretty—she graduated from the school of hard knocks and is challenging some of Ian's old-school ways. Could this dad learn some valuable lessons about love, family and faith from the least likely teacher?

Look for

Love Lessons

by

Margaret Daley

Available April wherever books are sold.

www.SteepleHill.com

Steeple Hill®

LI87590

HER MEDITERRANEAN PLAYBOY

Sexy and dangerous—he wants you in his bed!

The sky is blue, the azure sea is crashing
against the golden sand and the sun is hot.

The conditions are perfect for
a scorching Mediterranean seduction
from two irresistible untamed playboys!

Indulge your senses with these two delicious stories

A MISTRESS AT
THE ITALIAN'S COMMAND
by *Melanie Milburne*

ITALIAN BOSS,
HOUSEKEEPER MISTRESS
by *Kate Hewitt*

Available April 2010 from Harlequin Presents!

www.eHarlequin.com

HP12910

HARLEQUIN
Ambassadors

Want to share your passion for reading Harlequin® Books?

Become a Harlequin Ambassador!

Harlequin Ambassadors are a group of passionate and well-connected readers who are willing to share their joy of reading Harlequin® books with family and friends.

You'll be sent all the tools you need to spark great conversation, including free books!

All we ask is that you share the romance with your friends and family!

You'll also be invited to have a say in new book ideas and exchange opinions with women just like you!

To see if you qualify* to be a Harlequin Ambassador, please visit www.HarlequinAmbassadors.com.

*Please note that not everyone who applies to be a Harlequin Ambassador will qualify. For more information please visit www.HarlequinAmbassadors.com.

Thank you for your participation.

BAP09BPA

HARLEQUIN® *Romance.*

ROMANCE, RIVALRY
AND A FAMILY REUNITED

THE BRIDES
of
BELLA ROSA

William Valentine and his beloved wife, Lucia, live
a beautiful life together, but when his former love Rosa
and the secret family they had together resurface,
an instant rivalry is formed. Can these families
get through the past and come together as one?

Step into the world of Bella Rosa
beginning this April with

Beauty and the Reclusive Prince
by
RAYE MORGAN

Eight volumes to collect and treasure!

www.eHarlequin.com

HR17650

REQUEST YOUR FREE BOOKS!

2 FREE NOVELS PLUS 2 FREE GIFTS!

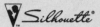

SPECIAL EDITION

Life, Love and Family!

YES! Please send me 2 FREE Silhouette® Special Edition® novels and my 2 FREE gifts (gifts are worth about $10). After receiving them, if I don't wish to receive any more books, I can return the shipping statement marked "cancel." If I don't cancel, I will receive 6 brand-new novels every month and be billed just $4.24 per book in the U.S. or $4.99 per book in Canada. That's a saving of 15% off the cover price! It's quite a bargain! Shipping and handling is just 50¢ per book in the U.S. and 75¢ per book in Canada.* I understand that accepting the 2 free books and gifts places me under no obligation to buy anything. I can always return a shipment and cancel at any time. Even if I never buy another book from Silhouette, the two free books and gifts are mine to keep forever.

235 SDN E4NC 335 SDN E4NN

Name	(PLEASE PRINT)	
Address		Apt. #
City	State/Prov.	Zip/Postal Code

Signature (if under 18, a parent or guardian must sign)

Mail to the Silhouette Reader Service:
IN U.S.A.: P.O. Box 1867, Buffalo, NY 14240-1867
IN CANADA: P.O. Box 609, Fort Erie, Ontario L2A 5X3

Not valid for current subscribers to Silhouette Special Edition books.

Want to try two free books from another line?
Call 1-800-873-8635 or visit www.morefreebooks.com.

* Terms and prices subject to change without notice. Prices do not include applicable taxes. N.Y. residents add applicable sales tax. Canadian residents will be charged applicable provincial taxes and GST. Offer not valid in Quebec. This offer is limited to one order per household. All orders subject to approval. Credit or debit balances in a customer's account(s) may be offset by any other outstanding balance owed by or to the customer. Please allow 4 to 6 weeks for delivery. Offer available while quantities last.

Your Privacy: Silhouette is committed to protecting your privacy. Our Privacy Policy is available online at www.eHarlequin.com or upon request from the Reader Service. From time to time we make our lists of customers available to reputable third parties who may have a product or service of interest to you. If you would prefer we not share your name and address, please check here. ☐

Help us get it right—We strive for accurate, respectful and relevant communications. To clarify or modify your communication preferences, visit us at www.ReaderService.com/consumerschoice.